ROSS O'CARROLL-KELLY

'I love him, but I'm not in love with him.

I certainly wouldn't, like, be with him again.'

Sorcha

'He's like Luke Skywalker and Han Solo rolled into one.

With a bit of Chewbacca as well.'

Christian

'He's the next Brian O'Driscoll. I said as much to

Gerry Thornley. Then he brought up that

barring order nonsense.'

Charles O'Carroll-Kelly

'The kid has no brain. But he has no conscience

either, so he's perfectly cut out for real estate.'

JP's old man

'One of the century's great thinkers.'

Fionn

Dedication

For Rich, Vin and Mark, my brothers

Acknowledgements

The publisher and the author wish to thank the **Sunday Tribune** for

permission to reproduce previously published material from the Ross O'Carroll-Kelly column.

Thank you to Rachel, Ger, Deirdre and Vin for the excellent editing job. Thanks also to Emma and Alan.

ROSS O'CARROLL-KELLY

The Orange Mocha-Chip Frappuccino Years

(As told to Paul Howard) Illustrations by Alan Clarke

THE O'BRIEN PRESS
DUBLIN

This edition first published 2016 by The O'Brien Press Ltd,
12 Terenure Road East, Rathgar, Dublin 6, D06 HD27, Ireland.
Tel: +353 1 4923333; Fax: +353 1 4922777
E-mail: books@obrien.ie
Website: www.obrien.ie
Previous edition published 2003, Reprinted 2003 (twice), 2004, 2005 (twice),
2006 (twice), 2007 (twice), 2009, 2011, 2012.

ISBN: 978-1-84717-841-1

1 3 5 4 2
16 18 20 19 17

Typesetting, editing, layout and design: The O'Brien Press Ltd
Illustrations: Alan Clarke

Printed and bound by Norhaven Paperback A/S, Denmark.
The paper in this book is produced using pulp from managed forests.

Published in:

DUBLIN
UNESCO
City of Literature

Contents

Introduction

They sem so long ago now, those *Orange Mocha-Chip Frappuccino Years.*

I wrote what was intended to be the third and final installment of the Ross O'Carroll-Kelly trilogy in the autumn of 2002, a period when the Irish Government was quite literally giving away free money, the entire country developed a fetish for timber decking and St Mary's College had a young, teenage out-half called Jonathan Sexton who was apparently going to be the next Ronan O'Gara.

It was also the year when a friend told me that he'd discovered his plumber snorting cocaine off the top of his toilet cistern at eleven o'clock in the morning. That's what I regard as the defining image of the period of temporary economic buoyancy that we refer to as the Celtic Tiger.

If you cared to look, there were a lot of signs that Ireland – much like the Rossmeister himself – was beginning to lose the run of itself.

I felt this very clearly at the time because I happened to be in the market to buy a house, having allowed myself to be convinced that it was somehow morally delinquent of me not to get myself onto the property ladder.

So I started visiting banks and lending institutions, the thought of which filled me with a quiet terror. In my youth, the bank manager was a figure of fear, an unsmiling, tyrannical character you only got to meet if you were in some kind of trouble.

But not in the autumn of 2002. By then, bank managers had been reimagined as good guys. They were cheery men in short-sleeved shirts, with no ties, who were desperate to lend you money and prepared to smile indulgently while you told them fib after barefaced fib.

I was informed by one mortgage adviser that I was 'debt-poor', which was an inversion of what I'd been brought up to believe. I thought that to have no debt whatsoever was to be rich, relative to, say, someone who owed the bank a million quid. These days, this is popularly held to be true again, but, in the autumn of 2002, that wasn't the case at all. I was 'debt-poor' but, happily, there was no shortage of financial institutions prepared to dig me out of that particular hole.

I was told how much I could borrow. It wasn't quite a million. But it still seemed to me an obscene amount of money, given the notoriously unreliable nature of the newspaper industry, in which I worked – particularly the newspaper that employed me at the time – and the fact that I was borrowing the money on my own.

But having received mortgage approval in principle, I struck out to look for a home to call my own. I spent the next few months viewing houses, apartments and greenfield sites that I was assured would one day be filled with houses and apartments.

I remember an estate agent showing me around a house that I quite liked in Greystones, County Wicklow. It was advertised as a three-bedroom house, but the third bedroom could have accommodated a bed only if you knew someone who enjoyed sleeping upright.

Batman would have loved it.

The asking price was €750,000 and that part of me that grew up in a council house that cost my father £11 per week to rent wanted to scream: 'Are you out of your mind?'

And of course he was – but there was a lot of it about.

He had narrow trousers, I remember, and impossibly pointy shoes and he seemed unnaturally young to be charged with the rather serious job of helping to sell people into a lifetime of crippling debt. I was quite confident that I had tins of food in my cupboard that were older than him. When I voiced my concerns about the size of the third bedroom, he laughed as if I'd misunderstood the entire point of the exercise, but misunderstood it in a way that was funny and adorable and would make a terrific anecdote later on.

'You're not going to live here forever,' he explained. 'You'll sell it in a couple of years for a massive profit and you'll move into an even bigger house.'

That was what passed food good sense at the time. In fact, our entire economy was founded on that shaky logic.

In the end, I didn't buy the £750,000 house. Perhaps I got scared. Or perhaps I just listened to that part of me that remembered Bono paying something very similar for a mansion on the Vico Road in Killiney just over ten years earlier.

The estate agent told me I'd regret it. I wasn't sure I would. But one thing I was absolutely certain about, as he hitched up his narrow trousers and prepared to give another prospective buyer the same pitch he'd given me, was that Ross O'Carroll-Kelly had to spend at least some part of his life working as an estate agent.

And this is what happened next.

Paul Howard, 2016

This friend of mine, roysh, he had a bit of a scenario with this bird. Portia was her name, roysh, met her in Annabel's, the usual craic, giving it loads, blah blah blah, ended up asking her out for dinner, which he wouldn't usually do, roysh, but she's actually a bit of a cracker – a better-looking version of Shannon Elizabeth – so he was prepared to put a bit of, like, spadework into the job. And anyway, roysh, the goys were all stood behind him, giving it, 'Crash and burn, crash and burn,' and this friend of mine, roysh, he was just there, 'Oh my God, I SO love a challenge.'

The only problem was, roysh, he didn't know where to bring her. He couldn't remember the last time he went out with a bird for dinner and he was like, 'What's a cool place to bring a bird these days?' And he must have really liked this bird because he decided he was going to pay for everything, none of this going halves bullshit. He ended up suggesting Roly's, roysh, which he regretted straight away because that's where his asshole of an old man usually goes, but as it turned out he needn't have worried, roysh, because the dickhead wasn't there.

And this friend of mine, roysh, he had to say that Portia

looked focking amazing this particular night. And the thing is, roysh, she was actually really nice this bird, as in a nice person and not just a lasher. And she storts, like, telling him, this friend of mine, all about herself as they're, like, looking through the menu. And, of course, he makes a total orse of himself. She says she's a vegan and he asks her how old she was when she moved to Ireland, but she just laughs and tells him she SO loves a goy with a sense of humour, and he can't make out whether she really thinks he was joking or whether she's just, like, embarrassed for me, I mean for this friend of mine. And it's only when she orders that he finds out that a vegan is someone who basically eats, like, grass and shrubbery.

But they get on well. She's actually really, really nice, which is usually a total turn-off for him. She tells him she does some work at night in the Simon shelter in town and, like, the dogs' and cats' home at the weekend, just helping with, like, feeding and shit, a real Princess Diana vibe off her. And he's really into her and she's really into him and it's, like, weird, but he thinks he might already be in love with this bird. She asks him about himself and he's like, 'Nothing much to tell,' and his steak arrives and so does her, like, cabbage, and she goes, 'I'm sure there is.' He's there, 'Well, I'm thinking of going back playing rugby. Had an offer from Clontarf and–' She goes, 'Hey, you can save the macho bullshit for the groupies in the Merrion Inn. I want to know the real you.' And he's speechless. He goes, 'The real me? Em … well, basically, Portia, I'm an asshole. I've always been an asshole. For as long as I can remember. I treat people like shit. Girls. Mates. The old pair. Don't know why. I'm basically not a very good person.' And she just, like, looks at him and goes, 'I think you're a good person.' He presses his fork into his steak and blood seeps out. He's like, 'Your friends, what did they say when they heard you were going out with me?' She goes, 'Honestly?' He's there, 'It's probably best.' She's like, 'They said I was mad. They said you were, well, all of the things you just told me you were.' He's there, 'And you still wanted to go out with me?' She goes, 'I'm one of those people who sees the good in everyone.' He's like, 'A bit of a Princess Diana vibe?' She laughs and goes, 'You can be yourself with me, you know.'

They go back to her gaff, a big fock-off apartment in, like, Blackrock, and she makes coffee and she goes, 'Sorry, there's no milk. Because I'm a—' He goes, 'Vulcan, I know,' and she breaks her shite laughing again and, like, punches him in the arm, all sort of, like, playful. And then, well, I don't have to paint you a picture, one thing leads to another, blah blah blah, and afterwards she goes, 'You're so much different to what people say,' and he goes, 'What people?' and she's like, 'Other girls.' And the next they know, roysh, they've both drifted off to sleep and after a few hours, roysh, he's woken up by this, like, beeping noise and it's his mobile and he realises he must have, like, fallen asleep. Portia, roysh, she's in the scratcher beside him and he gets out and grabs his phone, which is in the pocket of his chinos. And it turns out, roysh, that it's a text message from, like, Oisinn, one of the lads, and it's like, **WELL?** And this friend of mine, roysh, he thinks for a minute before he texts him back and when he does it's like, **HE SHOOTS! HE SCORES!** He looks at the clock and it's, like, three o'clock in the morning, and he didn't realise he'd been asleep so long. His phone beeps again and he reads the message and it's like, **UDM,** which is, like, **U DA MAN,** and then a few minutes later it beeps again and it's, like, **NOW GET DA FCK OUTTA THR.** He lies there in the darkness thinking for about half an hour, roysh, and then he gets up and puts on the old threads, trying his best not to wake Portia, but she does wake, roysh, and when she cops what's happening she goes, 'What are you doing?' And the goy, roysh, he goes, 'Going home.' And she's like, 'But there's no need.' He goes, 'Look, em … don't flatter yourself, okay. It was a one-night thing.' She goes, 'But you told me last night that you thought you–' and he goes, 'I know what I said. This is for the best. Believe me, Portia, you're too nice a chick. You really don't need someone like me in your life.'

And he walks straight out of there. Even though he really, really likes her, maybe even loves her, he gets the fock out of there. And you're probably wondering why. Because that's him. That's what he's like, this friend of mine. The goys call him The Tin Man. He has no feelings, that's what they say. Completely focking untouchable. In Annabel's, Lillies, Cocoon, every weekend you'll hear them all giving it that:

'Here comes Ross. The Tin Man.'

CHAPTER ONE
The One Where Ross Goes To D(twenty)4

I go to ring Fionn, roysh, to find out what the goys are doing for Hallowe'en night, but the old dear's already on the line, on the phone in the sitting room, dictating an ad for the paper and, like, giving the bird on the other end of the line a focking earful of abuse. I'm there on the extension in the kitchen, listening to her, roysh, and I have to put my hand over the mouthpiece to stop her from hearing me cracking my shite laughing. She's there, 'Cleaning Woman Wanted,' and the bird in the paper, roysh, she goes, 'Sorry, I have to stop you there. You can't be gender specific, I'm afraid.' The old dear's like, 'I beg your pardon,' and the bird's there, 'Gender specific. It's this new equality legislation, you see. You have to say, 'Cleaner wanted'.' The old dear's like, 'Yes, but you don't seem to understand. It's a *woman* I want to hire,' and the bird's there, 'Yes, but you have to be seen to offer men the opportunity to apply.' And the old dear storts going ballistic, roysh, she's there, 'I do not want some pervert going through my underwear drawer.' And the bird's like, 'I'm really sorry, I don't make the law.' The old dear, roysh, she's in a real snot at this stage, huffing and puffing down the phone. She goes, 'I suppose you have a problem with the next line as well. 'No Foreigners Need Apply'. I suppose you want me to change that to No Non-Nationals Need Apply, or somesuch.' The bird's like, 'Well, actually, you can't say either. Your advertisement can't be race specific.' The old dear's like, 'Oh for heaven's sake, this is political correctness gone mad,' and the bird goes, 'There's nothing I can do. I'm not allowed to–' The old dear's there, 'I am not hiring one of those refugees, if that's what you are getting at.' The bird goes, 'They're not my rules,' and the old dear goes, 'Romanian refugees? In *my* home? The very idea of it.'

✳ ✳ ✳

There's this game I like to play, roysh, where you see a good-looking bird out with her boyfriend – actually she doesn't even have to be that good-looking – but what you do is you catch her eye and try to, like, hold her stare until her boyfriend notices. I don't know why I get a kick out of it. I just do.

✳ ✳ ✳

Amy goes, 'I'm telling you, it's drinph,' and Faye, who's also first year law in Portobello, goes, 'Are you sure?' and Amy goes, '*Hello*? I think I know this subject better than you. You're the one repeating, remember?' I'm like, 'What the fock is drinph?' and Amy goes, 'It's D.R.I.N.P.H. They're initials, Ross. The duties of a receiver. Debts. Report. Interests. Negligence. Price. High Court.' I'm there, 'Am I, like, missing something here?' And Faye goes, 'We have a Christmas exam next week, and receiverships are SO going to come up.' Fionn, roysh, he pushes his glasses up on his nose, like he always does when he's about to show off, the focking brainbox, and he goes, 'I believe what's being referred to here, Ross, is the use of mnemonics as a means of retaining and then recalling large tracts of information.' What an asshole.

Amy is wearing a pair of black, knee-high Burberry boots, the old slut wellies, as the goys call them. She closes her eyes and goes, 'One, the receiver must pay the company debts in the correct order. Two, the receiver has a duty to report to the company, via the statement of affairs. Three, the receiver and debenture holder have a fiduciary relationship, i.e., the receiver must act in the best interests of the debenture holder regardless of whose agent the receiver is said to be, or the method of appointment. Four, the receiver is under a duty of skill and care and may be liable in negligence to the debenture holder and the company. Five, the receiver's main duty to the company is to get the best price available in the circumstances for the sale of the charge asset. Six, the receiver may apply to the High Court for directions in relation to any matter connected with the performance of his or her duties.'

I'm like, 'Sure, but what does it all mean?' And Faye's like, 'You don't need to know what it *means*, Ross. You just need to remember it. Oh my God, *how* did you manage to pass the Leaving?' Erika, roysh, the bitch, goes, 'He didn't,' and Faye just looks at me and goes, 'But you repeated it, like, twice?' and I go, 'I was on the Senior Cup team,' and I just, like, shrug my shoulders and go back to my chilli beef ramen. Amy goes, 'Okay, examinerships.' and Erika, roysh, she looks at her over the top of her shades and she's like, 'Excuse me, some of us aren't interested in this shit,' and Amy just looks her up and down and tells her she has an attitude problem, and Erika goes, 'Spare me,' calls the waitress over and orders another cappuccino, no a latte, no a cappuccino.

Oisinn arrives in, roysh, sits down next to me and makes this big, like, show of sniffing the air. Then he goes, 'Which one of you is wearing *Red Door*?' and no one answers, roysh, so he goes,

'As in Elizabeth Arden? Well, whichever one of you it is, be careful. I might try to hop you tonight.'

I turn on my phone. I have two voice messages. One from Rachael, this bird from second year science who I haven't seen since, like, the Traffic Light Ball last year and have no desire to ever see again. The other is from Michelle from Ulster Bank who'd like to arrange a meeting to, like, discuss my overdraft.

Erika all of a sudden goes, 'Hey, Fionn, how's Christian?' just basically being a bitch, roysh, and everyone at the table is suddenly looking at me. Fionn's like, 'He's, eh, he's great. There's a new *Star Wars* movie out next year, why wouldn't he be?' Erika goes, 'Have *you* seen Christian lately, Ross?' and I can actually feel my face going red. She's like, 'Oh no, of course, I forgot, he hasn't spoken to you since he found out about you and his mum.' I'm like, 'That is SO out of order,' and Amy's like, '*Hello?* Can we, like, change the subject here?' Fair focks to her.

Faye goes, 'Okay, okay, okay. Everybody, favourite 'Dawson's Creek' episode, we're talking *ever*?' Erika throws her eyes up to heaven. Amy goes, 'That's easy. The one where Dawson kisses Joey. *The sweetest, most romantic, Fourth-of-July-fireworky, waves-crashing-against-the-shore, beyond-any-movie-I-could-ever-imagine kiss.* Oh my God, SO romantic.' Amy and Faye are like focking clones of Sorcha, my ex who's gone to, like, Australia for a year. Faye goes, '*The hard part is over. We got through it. Fifteen years of preamble. Fifteen years of hyper-real dialogue disguising our most obvious feelings. It's all over now. The rest is simple. We'll make it simple.*' Erika just goes, 'Sad.'

Oisinn turns around and goes, 'Hey, you know which one I like best? The one where Jen and Joey get it on.' Faye's like, 'That never happened,' and Oisinn goes, 'Oh, you probably didn't see it. It was, like, a one-off. It was only shown late at night.' Faye goes, 'I think this may have been a dream you had?' and Oisinn's there, 'Which one of us hasn't? Are you sure you're not wearing *Red Door*?' Then he orders the tempura ramen, the ginger chicken udon and a chilli beef ramen, with side orders of steamed white rice and chillies, the fat bastard, and Amy goes, 'OH! MY! GOD! I SO love Japanese food,' roysh, and Faye goes, 'OH! MY! GOD! so do I,' even though I've never seen either of them actually eat it, or eat anything at all for that matter. Amy asks the waitress whether there's, like, celery in the yasai gyoza and when the waitress says yes she just, like, turns her nose up and says she doesn't want anything, and Faye, roysh, she just orders carrot juice and then basically picks food off my plate.

Eventually, roysh, Faye focks off to the jacks and when she's gone Amy goes, 'I'm not being a bitch or anything, but – OH! MY! GOD! – I cannot *believe* she thinks those trousers still fit her,' and she points out how much 'that girl' has put on since she came back from Montauk in the summer, and it's basically so sad the way she pestered her old man for membership of Crunch for her twenty-first and she's only used it, like, three times, and that's if you count going in the sauna and the jacuzzi as *using* a gym. I don't really know what Amy's bullshitting on about. Some birds, they wear those hipster trousers, roysh, and they've got those big trouser melons hanging over the waistband, but there's, like, fock-all meat *on* Faye. She comes back from the jacks, roysh, and says – OH! MY! GOD! – she feels like *such* a whale and she seriously needs to stort getting back to the gym, and Amy goes, 'Are those the trousers you wore to Eunan's twenty-first?' and Faye's like, 'Yeah, the ones I got in Karen Millen before the summer,' and Amy doesn't say anything back, roysh, and Faye gives her this filthy, like she knows she's being a bitch to her.

Then Amy storts talking about some dickhead who's on the permanent guest list in Reynards. Erika gets up to go, roysh, and Fionn's like, 'Are you not going to finish your coffee, babes?' He is SO trying to get in there it's not funny, as if she'd be interested in the geeky-looking focker. She goes, 'No, I'm going Christmas shopping with my mum. I said I'd meet her outside.' She gets her shit together, roysh, and she's about to leave, then she turns back and she goes, 'I'd bring her in to meet you all, but Ross might try to have sex with her.' And everyone at the table just breaks their shite laughing, roysh, and as Erika makes her exit they stop laughing and look sort of, like, embarrassed for me.

✱ ✱ ✱

I'm sitting at the kitchen table, roysh, in total focking ribbons, we're talking seriously hanging here, a feed of pints last night and a kebab on the way home, roysh, and my orse feels like the focking Japanese flag this morning. I know I should have put a toilet roll in the fridge last night. It's always too late when I think about it. And the old pair aren't helping matters, wrecking my head as usual. The old man's planning to go on the New Zealand tour with a few of his dickhead mates from the golf club next year, and he's going on and on and on about it. And the old dear, roysh, she's flicking through her speech for tonight's end-of-year residents' association meeting, highlighting important points with a yellow marker pen, totally ignoring the knobhead and I don't blame her. He's sort of, like, muttering under his breath, roysh, about Mount Cook and the Canterbury Plains, and all of a sudden, roysh, he has a sly look at the old dear to see if she's listening to him, and then he goes, 'Gerry Thornley's going.' The old dear looks up, roysh, over the top of her glasses, and she goes, 'Charles, please,' and he goes, 'I'm sure all that business is forgotten about,' and she's like, 'Charles, I do not want the police at the door again.' He's like, 'A misunderstanding is all it was. Gerry understands that now, I'm sure of it.'

I'm like, 'Will you two shut the fock up? I'm suffering here.' The old dear's like, 'Well, perhaps you shouldn't drink so much, Ross,' and I'm like, 'What are you, a focking doctor now?' and she goes, 'No,' and I'm like, 'Then drop the focking act.'

Then, all of a sudden, roysh, I realise that my mobile phone is gone, that it must have been, like, nicked in Soho last night and, to be honest, roysh, I'm not actually surprised, I was that ossified basically. Can hardly remember a thing. It was the usual crew, roysh, we're talking me, Oisinn, Fionn, JP and JP's cousin, Ryle Nugent, and we were all, like, knocking back the beers and giving it loads on the dance floor. Anyway, somewhere along the line, my phone must have been robbed, roysh, so I go into the sitting room, as far away as I can get from the two assholes, and I pick up the phone and dial my number, roysh. This total skanger answers it and basically, roysh, we're talking TOTAL here. He's like, 'Stor-ee?' I'm like, 'What the fock are you doing with my phone?' He goes, 'Alreet, bud. Good noyt lass noyt, wasn't it?' I'm like, 'One too many knackers out for my liking. What the fock are you doing with my phone?' He goes, 'Sorted. It's sorted, bud. Someone's after robbin' it on ye and Ine after gettin' it back for ye.' I'm there, 'Give it to me then.' He's like, 'It's gonna cost ye a finder's fee. Fifty squids, bud.' I'm like, 'I am SO not giving you money.' He goes, 'Then you'll never see yisser phone again.' I'm like, 'Alroysh, alroysh, you focking skanger. Where do I go?' Surprise sur-focking-prise, roysh, the goy lives in Pram focking

Springs, Tallafornia, and I tell him, roysh, that I'll give him a hundred bills if he comes out my direction and meets me at the Frascati Centre instead, but he's like, 'I'll meet you in de Square. In McDonald's. Next to the pictures. Four o'clock. And bring yisser money.'

So I phone up Oisinn, roysh, and I tell him the story and he goes, 'Ross, I can't let you do this alone,' which is what I was hoping he'd say, roysh, because the goy is a huge bastard. He's like, 'We'll get, like, a bit of a posse together to go with you.' So a couple of hours later, roysh, there we are in Oisinn's old man's Alfa Romeo, we're talking me, Oisinn, JP and Ryle, heading out to the northside or wherever the fock Tallaght is. I keep, like, nodding off, roysh, still majorly suffering from the night before, and I wake up at one stage and I'm, like, looking out the window going, 'Oh my God, what the fock is this place? Where have you brought us, man?' and Ryle's like, 'Calm down, Babycakes. Take it, like, easy,' and I'm there, 'Are you telling me people actually *live* like this? Oh the poverty, the squalor. It's focking inhuman,' and Ryle goes, 'Ross, this is Terenure. We haven't got there yet.'

But ten minutes later, roysh, we're in the middle of Tallaght and it's, like, a total Beirut buzz. JP goes, 'Oisinn, don't stop at any lights. They'll have the focking alloys off.' And Oisinn's like, 'TOTALLY.'

We get to the Square and pork, roysh, but it takes ages to find McDonald's. We're all wandering around this focking shopping centre, roysh, basically seeing how the other half lives, and it's all, like, Ken Ackers in twenty quid jeans and ninety quid runners trying to make eye contact with you for an excuse to kick the shit out of you, and AJHs in black leggings and bad perms, pushing prams around and going, 'Ah, Jaysus, Howiya.' It's a complete mare. We take a wrong turn and end up in, like, a pound shop and JP's there, 'Hair gel for a quid a tub? Somebody needs to hold a charity concert for these people.' And it's all tinsel Christmas decorations that poor people have hanging from their ceilings and, like, forty Christmas cards for a quid. And in the window of this other shop, there's this picture of, like, Jesus, one of those Sacred Heart jobs, roysh, and it's got, like, a clock built into the heart, and I think about buying it for my old pair, just to piss them off, but we're all, like, too tense to stort focking around. It's all about getting in, getting what you want and then getting out without being wasted, a bit like Tom Cruise in *Mission Impossible*.

Finally we find McDonald's. I go in and the goys are sort of, like, waiting around outside, keeping a discreet distance, waiting for the knacker to arrive. I see this goy with what looks like my Motorola V3690, totally staring me out of it, so I go up to him, roysh, and I'm there, 'Are you Anto?' He goes, 'Dat's me nayim.' I click my fingers and hold my hand out and go, 'Phone. Now.' He goes, 'Price has gone up, bud. Fifty squids … and yisser jacket.' I'm like, 'This is a focking Abercrombie.' He's there, 'I know what it fookin is, ye little poshie bastard. Gimme it.' I'm like, 'Yeah, roysh.' And he goes to stand up, roysh, but suddenly the goys are standing right behind me and Oisinn goes, 'Just give him the phone,' and the skanger, roysh, he's just about to say something when he cops Ryle and he goes, 'Here, aren't you dat fella what used to do 'The Grip'?' Ryle's like, 'Ten-four, Babycakes,' and the goy goes, 'Here, what's dat Jason Sherlock really like? I'd say he's sound as a pound, is he?'

Then everything happens really quickly, roysh. Oisinn uses the distraction to land one on the goy and totally deck him and there's, like, blood and curry sauce all over the place, and in the

confusion I grab my phone off the table, but all of a sudden, roysh, all these goys with Barry McGuigan moustaches a couple of tables down, they stort heading over, obviously the goy's mates, so we have to peg it pretty sharpish, the old rugby training paying off in the sprint back to the cor, which by some focking miracle still has all four wheels attached to it, and then we're all basically out of there. We're, like, SO out of there.

✳ ✳ ✳

I'm driving home from college, roysh, just broken up for the Christmas holliers, so I'm basically in great form, on the Stillorgan dual carriageway, cruising along in my cor – we're talking an 01 reg Golf GTI, black, alloys – minding my own business, when this focking bitch in a white Peugeot 206, roysh, decides to move into the fast lane all of a sudden without checking what was behind her, and she ends up nearly running me off the road, the stupid wagon. I wouldn't mind, roysh, but she's not even going fast enough to, like, be in the fast lane. I blare the horn at her, roysh, then drive right up her orse and stort, like, flashing my lights at her to freak her out and then, roysh, when we hit the next red light outside Foxrock church, I get out of the cor and go up to her and she winds down the window, roysh, and says she's really sorry. I'm like, 'Your mirror's not for checking whether you've got fake tan on your collar, you know.' She goes, 'Look, I'm sorry, I don't know what I was thinking.' And I'm like, 'Given that you're a bird, you were probably thinking about shoes.' She's like, 'What?' And I don't say anything else, roysh, just head back to my cor, which really pisses her off, because I can hear her still shouting back, 'What did you say?'

✱ ✱ ✱

Me and Christian, roysh, we hadn't spoken for ages and basically I can tell you that they were the worst months of my life. Then Christmas Eve, roysh, I'm in Kiely's, sitting at the bor, a few scoops in me, waiting for, like, Oisinn to arrive, when all of a sudden, roysh, Christian is suddenly sitting there beside me, as though nothing had, like, ever happened. He orders two pints of Ken without talking to me, roysh, then he goes, 'Ross, you know a thing or two about women, don't you?' I'm like, 'Christian, if this is about what happened between me and your old dear, I swear to you, she came on to *me*. Not being big-headed or anything, but basically—' He goes, 'I need advice, Ross.' He takes off his jacket, a black-and-red Henri Lloyd. I go, 'Hey, shoot.' He goes, 'There's this girl and, well … I think I've fallen in love with her.' I'm like, 'Hea-vy! Name?' He goes, 'It's Zam. Zam Wesell.'

I have to say, roysh, I've never actually heard of this bird, but I presume it's the German au pair his old man's got working for him, and if that's the case, roysh, then he needs more than advice, because his old man's been knobbing her for basically the last six months, or so the rumour goes. I'm like, 'How do you know it's love, Christian?' and he looks at me like I've got, like, fifty heads or something. He goes, 'You think I don't know what it feels like? I know what people say about me, Ross.' I'm there, 'You do?' He goes, 'Yeah. "Oh, he's just a vagabond space pirate, a mercenary spice smuggler with a death mark on his head."' I just nod. He goes, 'I might well be the fastest space pilot in the galaxy, Ross, but I'm also capable of feeling.' I'm like, 'I know, I know, I'm hearing you. It's just, like, you know, foreign birds, they're, like, different and shit.' He nods, roysh, as though I've said something, like, really deep, then he heads off for a slash.

Where the fock is Oisinn? I'm thinking. I realise my mobile is switched off. There's, like, something wrong with my battery. I lash it on again. Check my messages. Michelle from Ulster Bank called and wants me to call her back urgently. And Oisinn has also phoned to say he's going to be late because he's calling in to see *L'Air du Temps,* as he calls her, some bird he's seeing who works in the Frascati Centre. He goes to me last week, 'You should see this bird. She … is … focking … *huge,'* like he's really proud of the fact. The Chubby Chaser, the goys call him.

Christian arrives back and he goes, 'I used to be so different. Slapdash. Reckless. If I had everything in the world, I'd risk the lot on a half-decent sabacc hand. But now …' I'm like, 'Have you spoken to her?' He looks at me like I'm mad and shakes his head. He's like, 'You make it sound so easy.' I'm like, 'It is easy. Just walk up to her and talk to her, man. Ask her out to the flicks.' I order two more pints. He looks totally lost, roysh, and we're talking TOTALLY here. He goes, 'As if she'd be interested in a scruffy-looking nerf-herder like me.' I'm like, 'Christian, you've chatted up birds before.' He goes, 'Not like this one.' I'm there, 'What's so special about her?' He thinks for a minute, roysh, then he goes, 'Her eyes … I might write her a letter.' A letter, for fock's sake. I'm like, 'Not a bad idea.' He goes, 'Yeah, that way I can tell her exactly how I feel, like I've been waiting for her all my life and shit.' I'm like, 'Don't lay it on too thick, though. You want to knob this girl, but you also want to keep your options open.' He goes, 'No, Ross, I don't. She's the one.'

I don't know why, roysh, but I feel really, like, protective of the goy. I'm like, 'Christian, I don't want to see you get hurt here.' He goes, 'Hurt?' and I'm like, 'Look, are you absolutely sure your old man isn't – how do I put this – already in there?' He goes, 'My old man? And Zam Wesell? Ross, where the fock do you get your ideas from?' I'm like, 'They were seen, Christian. Holding hands. Coming out of The Queens. We're talking three weeks ago.'

He goes, 'Zam Wesell was in The Queens? You're bullshitting me.' I'm like, 'Christian, why do you think the goys call your old man Chris de Burgh?' He goes, 'What?' I'm like, 'Do I have to spell it out for you? He's banging the au pair.' And Christian's like, 'Hildegard? I know that. Everybody knows that. What's that got to do with Zam?' I'm like, 'Oh sorry, Christian. Our wires were crossed there. I thought … I thought Zam was the name of the German bird. Who's this Zam then? Where did you meet her?' He goes, 'I saw her for the first time on the cover of a magazine.'

I'm like, 'Bull*shit*. Are you saying she's a model?' And he looks me up and down again, like he's trying to work out what planet I've just come from, and he goes, 'Zam Wesell, Ross. ZAM WES-ELL. She's the bounty hunter in the new *Star Wars* movie.' And he pulls out this, like, movie magazine, roysh, with a picture of this bird on the cover, wearing these purple, like, motorbike clothes, a veil and a focking colander on her head, and she's, like, pointing a gun at the camera.

All of this sort of, like, catches me unawares, you have to understand. I want to tell him what a focking spacer he is, but I don't want to hurt the goy's feelings. And she *is* actually a bit of a lasher. He goes, 'You're not interested in her yourself, Ross, are you?' suddenly all, like, worried. I'm there, 'Christian, I won't get in your way. I can promise you that.' He nods. I can't believe I'm having this conversation. He goes, 'She might have a friend. For you, like. Wouldn't be as good-looking as her, of course.' I'm like, 'I don't mind. I'd take a bullet for you, Christian.' He takes a long drink out of his pint and neither of us says anything for ages. I can't believe I've got my best friend back. Best Christmas present I'll get this year. He goes, 'You mean laser blast, Ross.' I'm like, 'What?' He goes, 'You said you'd take a bullet for me. You mean laser blast.'

✱ ✱ ✱

Christmas. I do *not* want to talk about it. It was a real, like, family affair, roysh, the old pair, all lovey-dovey as usual – borf, borf – all presents and turkey and mulled wine and midnight Mass and mascarpone and charades and the Queen's speech and Baileys and Buckaroo and sherry focking trifle and Noel Edmonds and mind the Waterford Crystal and plum pudding and red candles and BT luxury crackers and *You Only Live Twice* and paper hats and bullshit conversation and Belgian chocolates and smoked salmon and asshole relatives and hot port and brandy butter and Charlotte Church and wrapping paper and 'Oooh, I love you so much, darling,' and pass the focking sick bag. I am SO not going to be here for it next year.

✱ ✱ ✱

Orlaith, this bird I know, roysh, works in a PR firm, Brown Nose and Schmooze Public Relations as we call it, she's a pain in the focking orse, roysh, but a ringer for Kate Beckinsale. She rings me on my mobile and storts telling me all about what a great New Year she had. She says that a bunch of them rented, like, a cottage on the Aran Islands, roysh, and OH! MY! GOD! you *should* have seen the state of Sara with no h, who drank, like, practically a whole bottle of vodka after Conor, her ex, ended up going off with, like, Keeva – *Hello*? – the girl who's supposed to be, like, her best friend. I pretty much switch off while this is going on, roysh, and when she eventually lets me get a word in edgeways, I'm like, 'So, what was the weather like?' Not that I actually *give* a shit, you understand. I'm just basically making conversation. Scoring Orlaith is, like, a long-term project of mine. She goes, 'It was okay. But there was no coverage, though. It was, like, SO frustrating not being able to text. And OH! MY! GOD! they changed over to the euro as well. I didn't think they would. Though I suppose the Aran Islands are pretty much Ireland, aren't they?' Then she's like, 'What are you doing tonight?' I'm like, 'Cinema. You?' She's there, 'Might go for a sauna later on. Hey, I met Faye and Amy in Crunch last weekend. On the sunbeds. Those two seem to be as thick as thieves.' And I'm just like, 'Yeah, cool.'

She goes, 'Speaking of cool, OH! MY! GOD! I saw your mum on Six-One.' I'm like, 'Yeah, making a total tit of herself as usual.' She goes, 'Oh my God, she SO didn't, Ross. I thought she was SO good. I didn't even know she was involved with the ... what do they call it?' I'm like, 'The Move Funderland to the Northside Campaign. A couple of her friends live in Sandymount, you see.' She goes, 'Some of Mum and Dad's do too, and oh my God, the knackers it brings into the area. Total CHV. It's like, OH! MY! GOD!' I'm like, 'Yeah.' She goes, 'Your mum is *such* a good speaker. What was it she said? "Funderland is fun for everyone – except if you happen to live in Sandymount." That was *such* a clever thing to say.' I'm like, 'Well, she is, like, PRO for the group.' She goes, 'And when she stood in front of that bomper cor, OH! MY! GOD! she was, like, SO brave.' I'm like, 'I wish it had focking hit her.' She's like, 'You can't say that, Ross. I mean, there's no room for something like Funderland in the New Ireland. Fair play to her for saying that to the gorda. I mean, why don't they put it in Ballymun? When they knock down all those, like, flats and shit.' I'm like, 'Yeah, maybe–' She goes, 'OH! MY! GOD! isn't your twenty-first coming up?' I'm like, 'Not until May.' She goes, 'Cool. What are you doing for it?' I'm like, 'Porty in the gaff, probably. The old pair are putting up, like, a marquee and shit. Should be cool.' She's there, 'Cool.' I'm like, 'Yeah, cool.' She goes, 'OH! MY! GOD! 'Sex and the City' is on tonight.' I'm like, 'Is that the one with the–' She's like, '*Lesbians, yes.* Oh my God, you are actually *worse* than Oisinn. Anyway, she's not a lesbian anymore. It was *actually* just a phase.'

The conversation is storting to bore the orse off me, roysh, but with girls like Orlaith you really have to put the work in if you're going to get anything out of it at a future date. She carries on blabbing for, like, twenty minutes about nights out she had over Christmas, roysh, and how she is turning into *such* a Samantha, whatever the fock that is, and she storts telling me about all these goys she was nearly with. *Nearly*, I stress. Orlaith, I've noticed, is never actually *with* anyone, which makes her a bit of a challenge. I chanced my arm with her in Tram Co one night about a year ago, roysh, she was basically coming on to me all night, so I moved in for the kill and she just, like, pulled away. I was like, 'Hey, you're being offered the chance to be with Ross O'Carroll-Kelly. Might not come around again.' She goes, 'No, I'm, em, seeing someone.' I'm like, 'Who?' She's there, 'Rob.' I'm there, 'Rob who?' She goes, 'Rob … O'Brien.' Now I may have failed the Leaving three times, roysh, but I'm not stupid. *Nobody's* called Rob O'Brien, that's the kind of name you make up when a copper catches you pissing up against an ATM in Donnybrook at four o'clock in the morning after an international match. So that was the night I put Orlaith's name alongside Erika's in the file marked, 'Long-term Projects.'

I turn around to her and I'm like, 'You must be looking forward to going skiing. I'm actually looking forward to seeing you again. I'm glad you're coming to my twenty-first.' Pretty smooth, I have to admit. She goes, 'Ross, I've told you before. You're too much of a bastard for my liking.' I'm there, 'I'm not anymore. I've changed … Orlaith.' I nearly said Erika. She goes, 'Sure you have.' I turn around to Fionn, who's sitting beside me, roysh, and I'm like, 'Fionn, haven't I changed?' And the next thing, roysh, I hear all these people going, 'Ssshhh,' and I turn around, ready to, like, deck someone. I'm like, 'WHAT is your focking problem?' Someone goes, 'We're trying to watch the film. You shouldn't even have that on in here.' It was Lord of the focking Rings. I'm like, 'Can you blame me? This is shit.' Then I go, 'Orlaith, I'm going to have to call you back.'

The next thing, roysh, this bird is suddenly shining a torch in my face and telling me and Fionn to get out. I'm like, 'With pleasure,' but Fionn, who was actually enjoying the film, believe it or not, is really pissed off with me, the specky focker. I'm glad to see one of us understood what the fock was going on in it. It was something like six hours long. I was growing a focking beard sitting there. As we're heading out, roysh, I think of something really funny to shout and basically I can't resist it, roysh, so I leg it back in, open the door and I'm there, 'We're closing up for the night out here. Turn off the lights on your way out. When it's finally over, that is.' Which you have to admit, roysh, is pretty funny. Fionn didn't think so, though. No sense of humour basically.

✳ ✳ ✳

Dickhead gets me tickets for the Ireland versus Italy match. He's like, 'They're on the mantelpiece, Ross, behind your mother's

John Rocha signature carafe.' I'm like, 'Am I supposed to be focking grateful or something?' Which I probably should be, roysh, but you give my old man the least bit of encouragement and suddenly he's trying to be all palsy-walsy with you, which basically I don't need at this stage in my life.

I meet Oisinn and a few of the birds before the game, roysh, just for a bit of lunch, but Erika's in one of her usual moods, just sitting there constantly sighing and, like, throwing her eyes up to heaven and she hasn't even touched her moyashi soba. Eventually, roysh, completely out of the blue, she goes, 'Is it just a coincidence that all the worst words in a woman's life contain the word 'men'? We're talking menstruation, we're talking menopause, we're talking–' Oisinn's like, *'Ménage à trois?'* And Erika, roysh, she gives him the finger and goes, 'In your dreams,' and me and Oisinn high-five each other, even though I don't speak German.

The waitress bird, roysh, who Erika's been giving filthies to all day, she brings the bill, roysh, drops it on the table and I'm straight out with the wallet, basically offering to pay for everything. I'm pretty much quids-in at the moment, and Aoife goes, 'OH! MY! GOD! you are *such* a life-saver. My cord is, like, SO maxed out after Christmas. I mean, *Hello?*' But Erika, roysh, she goes, 'What do you think you're doing, Ross?' and I'm there, 'Treating you to lunch,' and she, like, throws my money back across the table at me, roysh, and goes, 'We don't need you paying for our lunch. What *is* it about men?' She gets up, roysh, and goes to the jacks, followed quickly by Aoife and Jayne with a y, and Oisinn goes, 'Shit the bed, her difficulty with taking money from men obviously doesn't extend to her daddy,' and I'm like, 'She's just a bit hormonal, I'd say.' I reach across the table and grab her Discman and I look inside and it's, like, Destiny's Child, which explains a thing or two.

Oisinn eats everybody's leftovers, roysh, including the end of my yasai itameru, which I was planning to eat myself, but I say nothing, and we decide to head off before the chicks come back, hit Kiely's and throw seven or eight pints into ourselves before the game. The two of us sit up at the bor and Oisinn storts telling me that Break for the Border is a great place to go if you want to score ugly birds, and we're talking TOTALLY ugly here, and that before Christmas he was with this bird in there who looked like Colin Montgomerie, and I tell him thanks for the information.

In terms of, like, tipping us over the edge, roysh, it was the next four pints that did the damage. We were basically pretty much off our tits after about two hours and we didn't know whether we were playing Italy or … I don't know, some other country beginning with I, Iceland or Ithiopia. Getting focked out of Kiely's for singing meant we got to Lansdowne Road half an hour early, roysh, and we killed the time by going from one hospitality tent to the next, heckling all these dickheads who were making, like, speeches and shit.

We go into one tent, roysh, and there's this total knob in a suit, roysh, bullshitting on about how, as logistics and planning manager of whatever focking company he works for, he felt that in the current economic climate his business had much in common with the Irish rugby team. He's there, 'Maintaining consistency is vital if you don't want to continue existing off the glories of the past. And like the Irish goys, we're now under new management … and there are great times ahead.' I'm about to shout, 'Bullshit,' roysh, but Oisinn gets in before me with something even cleverer. He goes, 'If they're as focking boring as you, I'm asking for my money back,' which – surprise, surprise – only me and Oisinn find funny and one of the security guards focks us out.

We move on to the next tent, roysh, and there's a face I vaguely recognise up on the stage and he's there going, 'This Paddy Teahon business could be just the opportunity we've been waiting for to tell the Government what they can bloody well do with Knacker Park once and for all.' And everyone claps, roysh, and I squint my eyes to try to stop myself, like, seeing double, and Oisinn goes, 'Ross, isn't that your old man?' and I'm like, 'Let's go and find our seats, man.'

The match is a good laugh, what I can remember of it. Oisinn suggested doing a streak, and even though I knew deep down that it was a bad idea, roysh, I just kept thinking about it for, like, the whole game, that's how pissed I was, and I have to say I was pretty thankful for the fact that I couldn't stand up. That was the only reason I still had my shirt and, like, chinos on at the final whistle.

We stayed in our seats for, like, half an hour after the game, roysh, until we felt we could trust our legs again, then we staggered down the steps and down the back of the West Stand and, like, all of the players had storted coming out and were wandering back to the bus. And I remembered, roysh, that I still had this disposable camera in my pocket, the one that was left on our table at Philipa's twenty-first, so I pull it out, roysh, and I turn around to Oisinn and I'm like, 'Let's have some craic.' So we walk up to, like, Gary Longwell, roysh, and I hold up the camera and I go, 'Gary, any chance of a photograph?' and he goes, 'Sure.' So I hand him the camera, roysh, and me and Oisinn stand there in front of him with an arm around each other's shoulder and pose for a picture. It's focking hilarious. We do the same thing to

Girvan Dempsey, Ronan O'Gara and Simon Easterby, but not to Peter Clohessy. Best not to push our luck there.

So there we are, roysh, bursting our shites laughing over this, when all of a sudden this bloke comes over, I think I know the face, and he goes, 'The jealousy must be just eating you up, boy.' I'm like, 'Excuse me?' He goes, 'You're jealous. That's what all this is about.' I'm suddenly all defensive, roysh. I'm like, '*Meaning?*' He goes, 'Meaning that could have been you. You could have been wearing one of those green jerseys today and you know it.'

And I just walk off, roysh. Oisinn catches up with me and he asks whether I fancy going for a few more scoops, maybe back to Kiely's if they'll have us, but I tell him I'm, like, not in the mood anymore. And on the Dorsh, roysh, neither of us says anything, except at one point, between Sydney Parade and Booterstown, Oisinn turns around to me and goes, 'That was Eddie O'Sullivan, wasn't it?' and I'm just like, 'Cop on to yourself, Oisinn.'

CHAPTER TWO
The One Where Ross Is 21

'You won't ring me,' Muireann goes. 'I know you won't.' At least, I think her name is Muireann. She's there, 'Oh my God, that SO always happens when a goy gets it on the first night.' I give her a hug, roysh, and I'm there, 'Listen to me, I've got as much respect for you this morning as I did last night,' and I'm making a big zero behind her back, roysh, which is sort of, like, childish, I know, but it's something to tell the goys later. She pulls away from me, roysh, so she can look into my eyes – as if she's going to find something in them – and she goes, 'Giselle was, like, SO wrong about you.' I'm there, 'I'm glad to hear it,' playing it totally Kool and the Gang, hoping to get another quickie in before she heads off to work. But she's big into hugs this bird, roysh, and she's there giving me another, like she's never going to see me again. And although I haven't broken the news to her yet, she isn't. And I'm just standing there, roysh, praying that she doesn't move her hand down to my orse because I've got one of her CDs in my back pocket. It's a long story.

About six months ago, roysh, I storted this new craze called Petty Pilfering. Basically, every time you knob a bird you have to steal a CD from her bedroom. Anyway, without wanting to sound like a total dickhead, roysh, I've got nearly a whole shelf of them at this stage. Some of them are pretty decent as well, I have to say. We're talking Pulp's *A Different Class*, The Verve's *Urban Hymns* and the soundtrack from *Trainspotting*. Of course, Fionn has to, like, hijack the whole thing. He says that stealing CDs that you actually *want* means it's not a game at all, it's just thieving, which basically makes me a knacker. This all came out a couple of weeks ago in The Bailey, when I pulled out the new Oasis album, which I had snaffled from Elaine, as in Glenageary Elaine with the black curly teeth.

Fionn goes, 'Philosophically, Ross, you'd have to ask yourself whether you're doing this for fun, or if you're succumbing to some primordial instinct that's in you to take things that don't belong to you. Who knows, in a previous life you might have lived in Bray.' I was, like, so tempted to deck the focker, break every pane of glass in his face. Instead, roysh, I did what I do best. The next time he saw me, I laid OTT's *This One's For You*, Hootie and the Blowfish's *Cracked Rear View* and *The Best of Andrew Lloyd Webber* down on the table and went, 'Alisa from LSB, Katy from the tennis club and Simon's cousin with the huge baps who used to work in Benetton. Read 'em and weep.' Of course, he doesn't know what to say. He's there pushing his glasses up on his nose going, 'Ross, I didn't mean to impugn ...' I'm just like, 'Notches on the bedpost, Fionn. Notches on the bedpost.' I know for a fact, roysh, that the second I left the boozer he was telling everyone that I bought them myself, which is total bullshit. He knows I did the business, roysh, with a bit of help from Hugo Boss, who makes jeans with a back pocket that fits a CD, like, perfectly.

So anyway, roysh, back to Muireann. I'm there going, don't let those hands go too low. Of course, the girl can't help herself. She, like, grabs my orse, roysh, and she's like, 'What's that?' I'm like, 'What?' She goes, 'In your pocket. What is it?' Quick as a flash, roysh, I'm like, 'It's, em, a present. It's a present for you. A CD.' She's like, 'Which one?' I can't even remember which one I robbed. I was going to take Madonna's *Something to Remember*, but couldn't decide whether it could be classed as cool or not. Anyway, roysh, I whip the CD out and straight away she's like, 'Gary Barlow. *Oh* my God!' Gary focking Barlow, that was it. I'm still there playing it cool as a fish's fart. I'm like, 'I hope you haven't got it already.' I know what's coming next. 'Em, no,' she lies. She's like, 'I've always wanted it though. OH! MY! GOD! You are *such* a mind-reader. You know me SO well.' Then she's like, 'This is probably *such* an uncool thing, but I prefer Gary Barlow to Robbie Williams. Oh my God, you SO better not tell Jenny and Esme that.' I would except I haven't a focking clue who she's talking about. I'm there, 'Yeah, well, I'm actually a Gary Barlow man myself.' If the goys find out I said that …

She takes the CD out of the box and, like, turns around to put it on and she goes, 'What's your favourite song?' and I scan down through the track list, picking songs at random. I'm like, ''No Commitment', 'Are you Ready Now?' 'I Fall So Deep', 'Forever Love'.' She goes, 'OH! MY! GOD! 'Forever Love'. That's *my* favourite as well. Oh my God, we are SO well suited.' So suddenly it comes on, roysh – *'My love it has so many empty spaces'* – and I'm there thinking, Like your head, Muireann. Just like your head. I don't actually say it, though. She gives me another hug and we stort, like, slow-dancing in her kitchen. What a sap. Wetter than a bank holiday weekend in Dingle. But I think there's a reasonable chance I'm going to get that quickie now.

Might take the Madonna CD after all.

✳ ✳ ✳

Aoife says that to burn off the calories from a Snickers bar would basically take forty-five minutes on an exercise bike, and Sophie goes, 'Oh my God! That's, like, OH! MY! GOD!' And Keera, roysh, she asks how long a Caramel bar would take and Aoife looks at her as though it's, like, the stupidest question she's ever heard in her life and she goes, 'How the fock would I know? What am I, an expert on dieting or something?' and Keera, like, shakes her head and goes, 'Sorr-ee!' and Aoife tells Keera she has *such* an attitude problem. Sophie says she went to the gym last night with Amy and Faye for a jacuzzi and one of those high-protein shakes.

I eat the froth at the bottom of my cup, lick the spoon and check my messages. There's, like, two. One is from Eva who wants to know whether I've heard about Anna, not Anna as in first year law Portobello Anna but Anna as in clarinet Anna, and the total fool she made of herself in the rugby club last Saturday night. Michelle from Ulster Bank has also rung to say she's, like, concerned about my overdraft, roysh, and I'm tempted to ring her back and tell her I'm glad one of us is because basically I couldn't give two focks.

Keera stands up, roysh, and makes a little announcement – she's going to the Ladies – and she says it, roysh, as though she expects Aoife and Sophie to come with her, but they don't move and Keera's already up on her feet, roysh, so she's sort of, like, past the point of no return you could say, and she has to go on her own. When she's gone, roysh, Aoife goes, 'Sorry, *how* much weight has that girl put on?' Sophie goes, 'I know, I know. It's like, OH! MY! GOD! It's like, *Hello*?' Aoife goes, 'Tell me that's a skinny latte she's drinking,' and Sophie's like, 'It's, like, SO not. It's, like, full-fat milk.' And Aoife goes, 'OH! MY! GOD!, that girl is, like, so … duuhh!' Sophie goes, 'TOTALLY. It's, like, her points have SO gone out the window since she broke up with Eoin. If she's, like, eating out, she only counts whatever she orders herself. If she, like, takes a few fries off your plate or has, like, half your dessert, it's like she thinks it doesn't count.' Aoife's there, 'That is SO, like … aaaggghhh!' and Sophie goes, 'I know. It's, like, totally … duuuhhh!' Aoife's there, 'It SO is. I'm, like, *Hello*?'

Keera comes back, roysh, and Sophie goes, 'Oh my God, Keera, you have lost SO much weight,' and Keera, like, looks at Sophie, then at Aoife, then at Sophie again, like she can't work out whether she's being, like, a bitch, and she eventually goes, 'I SO haven't. I look in the mirror and it's, like, OH! MY! GOD! I'm just like … aaaggghhh!' Sophie tells her she SO should wear that pink belly top she bought in Morgan for Críosa's twenty-first. Aoife tells her she SO should, that it would look, like, SO cool.

Fionn comes in, roysh, and it's, like, a relief to have some male company at last. Aoife and Sophie and Keera all stand up and, like, hug and air-kiss him, and Sophie tells him she has SO missed him and Fionn pushes his glasses up on his nose and goes, 'I met you in Benetton half an hour ago.' Aoife goes, 'OH! MY! GOD! Speaking of Benetton, Jane texted me this morning and she said Sara is SO not going out this weekend.' Sophie goes, 'Oh my God, that's, like, why not?' And Aoife goes, 'OH! MY! GOD! She was *such* a total slut last weekend. She was, like, flirting her orse off with Conor. All night. In the rugby club. We're talking Conor as in might be playing for the Clontarf J2s next year Conor. But she ended up being with, like, his best friend. We're talking Cian. It's, like, OH! MY! GOD!' Keera goes, 'That's, like, SO not a cool thing to do. It's like … duuuhhh!' Aoife goes, 'TOTALLY. It's, like … aggghhh.'

Sophie goes, 'That girl has turned into *such* a Samantha. It's, like … *Hello?*' Aoife goes, 'Oh my God, *I* am, like, a total Samantha myself. We are talking, like, OH! MY! GOD!' And Sophie goes, 'No, you're not. You're, like, Ally McBeal. You SO don't know what you want.' And Keera goes, 'And you are SO Joey from 'Dawson's Creek' as well,' and Sophie's like, 'Oh my God, TOTALLY,' and Aoife, roysh, she actually looks quite pleased with that.

I ask Fionn how college is going and he says fine, his course is a piece of piss. Sophie goes, 'OH! MY! GOD! What do you think of Monica's hair?' and me and Fionn, roysh, we look at each other, wondering who the fock Monica is, but we cop it when she storts, like, talking about Rachel and Phoebe as though she knows them. Aoife goes, 'I would SO like my hair like Rachel's. It's, like, SO cool. I'm like, OH! MY! GOD! I asked my hairdresser to, like, do my hair like hers and I looked in the mirror afterwards and it was like … aaaggghhh!' Sophie goes, 'I know, but that girl who did your hair, she has *such* an attitude problem. She is, like, SO … duuuhhh!'

Fionn goes, 'In a hundred and fifty years time everyone in Ireland will talk with an American accent. That's my prediction.' All the girls are like, '*Hello?* Where is this, like, coming from?'

Fionn and his theories.

✷ ✷ ✷

We only really sent Oisinn's name into 'Blind Date' as a joke, roysh. We came up with the idea one night when we were all watching it totally ossified in Fionn's apartment, so we downloaded the application form off the internet and filled it in without Oisinn knowing anything about it, never thinking of course that of all the millions of applications they get in that they'd pick his out. Anyway, they did, roysh, and he rings me up one afternoon and he's like, 'Ross, what the fock is going on?' and I'm like, 'Come on, Oisinn, it'll be a laugh. No, it'll be a lorra, lorra laughs,' and I basically say it the way that focking kipper says it. He's like, 'They want me over in London the day after tomorrow,' which is basically Paddy's Day, roysh, and I'm there, 'Hey, I'm with you. Every step of the way. We'll all go over.'

But basically, roysh, it takes me, JP, Fionn and Christian to persuade the dude to go over for the laugh, roysh. So the five of us head for the airport, roysh, check our bags in and, of course, hit the bor. So there we are, roysh, seven o'clock in the morning, basically skulling pints and we end up nearly missing our flight. JP's there telling us we need to take a helicopter view of the situation and we're all trying to work out what the fock he's talking about when all of a sudden, roysh, we hear our names called out over the intercom thing, and it's like, 'Please make your way to boarding gate 4B. Your flight is about to close.'

So we leave our pints there and peg it down to the gate, roysh, basically knocking people out of the way as we go, and we're pretty much there, roysh, when I realise there's only, like, four of us and we've lost Oisinn somewhere along the way. I tell the goys to get on board and I'll go and look for Oisinn, and Christian goes, 'No, Luke, it's too dangerous.'

Where else am I going to find Oisinn than the duty free shop, roysh, chatting away to the bird behind the perfume counter. I'm like, 'Fock's sake, Oisinn. We're going to miss the flight.' He grabs me by the arm, roysh, and storts sniffing the air. I'm like, 'We don't have time for this.' He goes, 'Can you smell that?' I'm like, 'Oisinn–' He goes, '*Green Tea*, Ross. It's Green focking Tea. Who else but Elizabeth Arden would come up with the idea of bottling tea and selling it to birds for twenty quid a pop.' He shakes his head. He's like, 'Genius.' I'm there, 'Oisinn, you're trolleyed.' And the bird behind the counter, roysh, mid-twenties maybe, looks a bit like that Kimberly Davies who used to be in 'Neighbours', caked in slap, she's like, 'No, your friend is right. It's a crisp, exhilarating fragrance that energises the spirit,' and I look at her, roysh, and I look at Oisinn, and I know that they've both basically found love here today, and it pains me that I have to basically drag the two of them apart.

As we're pegging it down to the boarding gate, Oisinn's going, 'I wanted you to get your nostrils around *Organza*, Ross. Givenchy's ode to the eternal woman, a scent with a velvety and mythical seduction.' Of course, he's still bullshitting on about this while I'm trying to persuade the birds at the gate to let us onto the plane. They're there going, 'Sorry, the gate is closed,' and I'm like, 'Hey, we've got a television show to record,' and I stort telling them all about, like, 'Blind Date', roysh, and I have to say, I think one of the birds has the serious hots for me, so in the end they let us on.

As we're walking down the aisle, roysh, the rest of the goys are down the back giving it loads, cheering and chanting our names, while everyone else on the flight gives us, like, total filthies, and we're talking totally here. We sit down, roysh, and then a minute later we're in the air and knocking back the beers again. At one point Oisinn turns around to me and goes, 'You didn't even give me a chance to get her number, Ross,' and I'm like, 'She wasn't your type.' He's like, '*Wasn't my type?*' and I'm there, 'Yeah, she was thin and she was good-looking.' He shrugs his shoulders and goes, 'You can't have everything.' I distract his attention when the duty free trolley rolls by, roysh, but JP, the shit-stirrer, he buys him a naggin of, like, Glenfiddich and Oisinn focking necks the thing, and basically it's from that point that the day storts to go out of control.

We land in London, roysh, and collect our bags. Oisinn, egged on by JP, decides to, like, sit on the carousel and go for a ride, while Fionn is chatting up some total stunner, telling her that he's always liked Jung's view of libido as an asexual, primal energy and he's there giving it, 'That's where both of us differ from Freud,' and the bird, roysh – I can't focking believe it – she's writing down her number on the back of Fionn's boarding pass, the nerdy-looking sap. And Christian, well, Christian's away in his own world, as usual, so it basically looks as though I'm going to have to take charge.

I drag Oisinn off the carousel, roysh, then we grab the bags and head on through and – fair focks to Cilla – there's, like, a limo waiting to pick us up and shit. So we all pile into the back and it's, like, an hour between the airport and the studio and we spend the time getting totally lubricated, roysh, because there's a whole focking drinks cabinet in the back, and there we are knocking back the VSOP brandies and smoking these big cigars and Oisinn is telling Christian about *Green Tea* by Elizabeth Arden and Christian is nodding really, like, thoughtfully, and I go, 'Lads, do you not think we should lay off the sauce a bit until after the show?' and they all just look at me, roysh, for ages, then they break their shites laughing and I laugh as well and pretend it was a joke.

We hit the studio, roysh, and we're all, like, herded into this, like, hospitality room, which is full of all the other, well, basically wankers who are going to be on the show. This big, English dickhead who thinks he's It, but he's basically a fat-headed rugby jock with no brain, he comes over and shakes our hands and tells us he was in Dubbalin once for a stag. Great city. He goes, 'Bladdy 'ell, you Irish know how to drink, what?' and Fionn mutters something like, 'That's such a stereotype,' and the English goy goes, 'Eh?' and Fionn doesn't say anything else.

The other goy who's going on is, like, Scottish, roysh, he's with a couple of mates of his and he's basically keeping himself to himself, and he's wearing – surprise sur-focking-prise – a kilt. JP goes, 'Saves them having to chat up birds. It's like when they come over for the rugby internationals. The birds just come up to them and go, "What do you keep under there?" Very sad. But the birds, well, they fall for it every time.' I'm like, 'You shouldn't have given Oisinn that whiskey. The goy can hardly stand. He's not going to be able to think up funny answers for the questions.' He winks and goes, 'Makes it a win-win situation as far as I'm concerned.'

The next thing, roysh, this producer comes in and goes through the, like, format of the show with us, but we've all watched it before. Then the three goys are asked for their answers to the three questions that the bird is going to ask them, roysh, which is when I find out for the first time that the whole show is, like, scripted. Bit of a disappointment actually. Oisinn manages to get his answers out and they're, like, pretty cringey it has to be said, although I've seen him score with worse lines.

Then Cilla comes in and she's amazing, roysh, tells all the goys not to be nervous, it's going to be fun – 'a lorra, lorra fun' – and remember to just be themselves, that's what the public wants to see. It's the last thing that Oisinn needs to be told.

The next thing we know, roysh, he's dragged off with the two dickheads to get the old make-up put on, and me and the goys are put sitting in the front row. There's a bit of a cheer from the rest of the audience, roysh, when they see we're all wearing our old Castlerock jerseys and we're there giving it, 'YOU CAN'T KNOW THE ROCK. YOU CAN'T KNOCK THE ROCK,' until the floor manager comes over and tells us to, like, settle down.

Christian tells me he's so nervous he feels like he's just staked the Naboo Royal Starship on the outcome of the big pod race on Boonta Eve, and then the music storts up, roysh – it's like, *Doo-Doo, Doo-Doo-Doo-Doo-Doo, Doo-Doo* ... – and Cilla comes out, roysh, and when the applause dies down, she's there, 'Well, chucks, have we got a show with a real British Isles feel to it this week. Our first contestants are an Englishman, an Irishman and a Scotsman,' and there's loads of, like, laughter from the audience, and she goes, 'It's norra joke, chucks,' and everyone breaks their holes laughing again and JP turns to me and goes, 'She's the consummate professional, isn't she?' She goes, 'So without further ado, let's meet our lovely lads. Tell us, number one, who are you and where do you come from?' The English goy's like, ''Ello, Cilla. My name's Scott and I'm from Dagenham,' and the audience go wild, roysh, even though it's probably a shithole. Cilla asks him a whole load of boring shite, then moves on to the second goy and he's like, 'Hiya doon, Cilla. My name's Andy and I'm fae Edinburgh,' and there's loads of, like, whooping and, like, hollering in the audience again. She throws in a few questions – 'What do you keep under there, chuck?' – and then she moves on to number three and I'm looking at the goy, roysh, and he's trying to focus on Cilla, but his eyes are, like, totally gone, but he does manage to get the words out, he's there, 'I'm Oisinn. I'm from Ballsbridge and Castlerock rules.' Big cheer from the front row. Cilla's like, 'Oooh, a rugby player. You've got some of your team-mates with you here today as well.' He gives us the thumbs-up and we're all like, 'Go, Oisinn. Go, Oisinn.' Cilla turns to the audience and she goes, 'Now, Oisinn, your friends tell me that you're something of a connoisseur when it comes to ladies' perfume, is that right?' And Oisinn's like, 'That's right, Cilla. And can I just say, I don't care if people say Chanel No 5 is passé, it's a classic fragrance that combines traditional accords with fresher, more modern notes.' Cilla's like, 'Chanel No 5, he's right ladies and gents,' and everyone laughs and Cilla goes, 'Oooh, that Irish accent. Makes you all goose-pimply, doesn't it,' and everyone laughs again. JP was right. What a professional.

Fionn leans over to me and goes, '*Result!* Cilla likes him. When Cilla likes you, it's like getting the thumbs-up from a bird's mother. It's cruise control all the way now. He just has to avoid saying anything stupid.' Cilla goes, 'Now let's meet the lovely lady who'll be going out with one of these lucky, lucky lads on a blind date. She's gorgeous and she's from Wales. Come in Claire,' except the way she says it, it sounds like Clur. So Clur comes in, roysh, and I have to say she's a focking stunner – we're talking Molly Sims here – and Oisinn's sort of, like, looking at us to get our reaction and me and JP make, like, gyrating motions with our hips. Cilla's like, 'Oooh, you've lovely hur, Clur,' and Clur's like, 'Thank you. I take after my mum,' thick as a focking ditch obviously. Cilla goes, 'What do you work at, Clur?' and she goes, 'I'm a credit controller with a LEADING CERAMICS MANUFACTURER!' and everyone cheers and claps as though it was something worth cheering and clapping about. Cilla goes, 'And what do you do in your spur time, Clur?' and Clur goes, 'Look for love.'

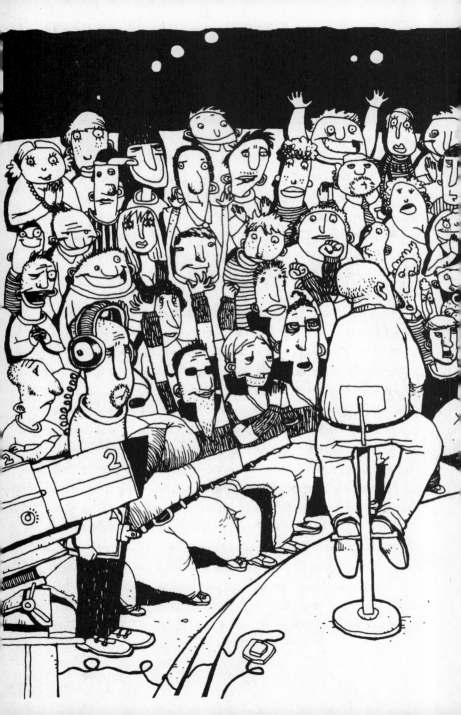

Cheer! Cilla goes, 'What do you look for in a man, Clur?' and Clur's like, 'Sensitive. Funny. Good-looking' – Oisinn has his work cut out, JP helpfully points out – and Cilla goes, 'Oooh, she's not fussy, is she, chucks? Well, we've got three lovely lads behind that screen and I'm sure you're going to have a helluva hard time choosing between them.'

Then it all storts to go wrong. I'm looking at Oisinn, roysh, and I know from his eyes that he's totally horrendufied at this stage, and we're talking TOTALLY here. And this Welsh bird, roysh, she goes, 'I am quite a confident and outgoing person and I often like to make the first move in relationships. If I approached you in a bar and asked you for a light, what would you say? That question to number one.' And the English goy, roysh, he's like, 'Hello, Clur. Well, if you was to ask me for a light, I'd probably ask you where you get your energy to light up a cigarette and the room at the same time.' And Cilla and the Welsh bird, they look at each other, roysh, and they're going, 'Oooh, yeah, not bad.' Next it's the Scottish goy. The bird goes, 'Same question to number two, please.' He's there, 'Hello, Clur. If ya came up tae me in a pub and asked me for a light, I'd probably say excuse me while I go ootside and pick one ay the stars outae the sky for ya, doll.' And Cilla and her are there going, 'Oooh, it's already so difficult to choose.' Then she goes, 'And number three, same question.' And Oisinn, roysh, he gets down off the high stool and he staggers forward and you can see, like, the producer and the floor manager and everyone else, they want to stop him but it's like they're frozen to the spot. And there's, like, total silence in the audience, roysh, and he walks around the other side of the screen and you can, like, see the shock on Cilla's face, and on Clur's as well, but it's nothing compared to the shock they're about to get, when Oisinn goes, 'If you asked me for a light … I'd say I've no matches …' – while he's saying this, roysh, he's unbuttoning his chinos and whipping out his lad – '… but how does *this* focking strike you?'

All hell breaks loose, roysh, and basically, to cut a long story short, we're all focked out of the studio, Oisinn shouting his head off, giving it, 'The bird was a dog anyway,' as these, like, bouncers drag him out of the place and throw him out on the road. No limo back to the airport either. And believe it or not they end up not showing it on television.

✳ ✳ ✳

I get up really early on Monday, roysh, grab a bowl of cornflakes, catch the end of 'Neighbours' and then go looking for the old man, who's, like, in the study, bullshitting away to one of his asshole mates on the phone. He's there going, 'A levy, Hennessy. On plastic bags. Never mind your Lawlors and your whatnots, this is a scandal and you won't be reading about it in your *Irish Times*.'

I've been standing in the doorway for, like, five minutes, basically trying to catch the knobhead's attention, so eventually I just go, 'Are you focking deaf?' and he's like, 'Just a second, Hennessy,' and he turns around to me and he's like, 'Hey, Kicker. What's up?' I'm like, 'Deaf *and* stupid. *Hello*? I'm doing my driving test again today.' He goes, 'That came around quickly. Doesn't seem like two years since you applied. Well, best of luck,' and he goes back to talking again. He's there going, 'The shop girl, she said it had nothing to do with Superquinn. No point getting angry with her, she said. Something to do with the environment. It's like that bloody National Car Test business, Hennessy. Using people's concern for the planet to extort more money out of them. Well, I told her. For every bag that these so-called Department of the Environment people ask me to pay for, I'm going to buy a can of deodorant, step outside the shop and spray it into the air. My wife is right behind me on this, so are the chaps from the club and I need you on board, Hennessy. I need you, that's absolutely mandatory with a capital M. Great big CFC parties in the car park of the Frascati Centre. And we'll see Bertie's face when there's a bloody great hole in the ozone layer over Dun Laoghaire. How do you like that, Mister Stadium?'

I'm like, 'Will you shut the fock up and listen to me?' He puts his hand over the mouthpiece and goes, 'Ross, please, I'm talking politics here.' I'm like, 'And I'm late for my driving test. I need a hundred bills.' He's there, 'But didn't I pay for the test when you applied? What do you need a hundred euros for?' I'm like, 'To focking celebrate. What do you think?' He hands me the shekels like it's a big focking struggle for him, roysh, then he goes back to talking shite and I head off, making sure this time to switch off my mobile because I think that may have had something to do with me failing last time. I'm actually not that orsed about sitting it again, roysh. The old man pays my insurance, so it's no skin off my nose whether it's four grand a year or forty. But the fockers won't give me a third provisional unless I, like, sit it again, so this time I didn't make the mistake of applying to do it in Wicklow. Everyone says it's a piece of piss to pass it in a bogger test centre, roysh, but actually it's not, so this time I lashed my application in for Rathgar. And basically, roysh, I was pretty well prepared. Drove the test route a couple of times with Christian the night before and did a serious amount of cramming for the whole, like, quiz part of the test. And I'm pretty confident I'm going to pass, roysh. That is until the examiner walks out.

I don't know the goy's name, roysh, but I went out with his daughter a couple of years ago. Didn't end well. Never really does with me. She was pretty alroysh looking, I have to say, went out three or four times and got on fine, until this one particular day, roysh, when we were driving back to her gaff after being at the cinema and she said those dreaded words: 'I don't believe in sex before marriage.' I basically told her to get the fock out of the cor. Don't get me wrong, roysh, I pulled over first. She was there, 'Ross, I live miles from here.' And I was like, 'There's a bus stop over there. Use it.'

I admit it was a pretty shitty thing to do – I hope I've grown up a bit since then – and it probably explains why her old man is so, like, hostile to me when he's asking me the questions. It's like, 'What's the speed limit on a national road?' I'm like, 'Ninety?' He goes, 'In a built-up area?' I'm like, 'You'd want to be dropping down to about sixty, sixty-five.' Then he goes, 'How do you approach a yellow box?' This focker would give Anne Robinson a run for her money.

We go out and basically I ace the test, roysh, except for this one T-junction where I make the mistake of pulling out without, like, looking both ways and this stupid bitch in a red Ford Mondeo hits her brakes and then storts, like, beeping me. But it doesn't matter, roysh, because the goy's already made up his mind to fail me. And then I go and make my second mistake. We're pulled up at the lights on Kimmage Road and I'm there, 'How's Elmarie?' letting him know that I know his daughter in the hope that it'll give me, like, an advantage, then realising that if she told him the full story, I'm focked. He doesn't answer. Doesn't even look at me, and I SO regret saying it.

He goes, 'Turn right here, then take the first right and show me your three-point turn,' like he's trying his best not to lose his cool with me. I'm so flustered, roysh, that I miss the turn and he storts, like, going apeshit. He's there, 'I TOLD YOU TO TURN! CAN YOU NOT FOLLOW BASIC INSTRUCTIONS?' I'm like, 'Hey, chill out.' He goes, 'Take the next left onto Whitehall Road!' I take it perfectly, roysh, but not perfectly enough for him. He's like, 'DO YOU KNOW WHAT YOUR INDICATORS ARE FOR?' I'm like, 'There wasn't anyone behind me.' He goes, 'YOU'RE SUPPOSED TO INDICATE AT ALL TIMES!' I'm like, 'Hey, I'm just about focking sick of the negative vibes you've been giving me.' He goes, 'Return to the test centre,' like a focking robot. I'm like, 'No, you listen to me. You had it in for me the second you laid eyes on me.' He goes, 'Return to the test centre. Now.' I'm like, 'What, so you can tell me I've failed? Fock that. Get out of the cor.' He goes, '*What?*' I'm like, 'Get the fock out of my cor. Now!' I reach across him, roysh, pull the handle on the passenger door and push it open. I'm like, 'Get the fock out.' And that's when I realise, roysh, that it's only, like, around the corner from where I threw Elmarie out, which is, like, such a coincidence it's not funny. He goes, 'The test centre is miles away.' And I'm like, 'Well, you know what I told your daughter.'

✳ ✳ ✳

We're in college, roysh – in theory I'm still repeating first year sports management in UCD, though I've only been to, like, four lectures since last September – and we're knocking back a few beers in the bor and Críosa, this bird who's, like, second year commerce, she asks me to go and get her smokes. So I head down to the shop, roysh, and I'm like, 'Twenty Marlboro Lights.' And the bird behind the counter, roysh, she's there, 'Excuse me?' I'm like, 'Marl-bor-o Lights. Twen-ty.' And I know what her game is, roysh. Basically, she wants me to say please. She gets them, roysh, puts them down on the counter and she tells me it's, like, eight euros or nine euros or whatever the fock they cost and I hand her a ten euro bill, roysh, and when she, like, gives me my change she goes, at the top of her voice, 'THANK YOU.' I'm just like, 'Thanks,' and as I'm walking out of the shop I can hear her going, 'That didn't hurt, did it?' Wench.

✷ ✷ ✷

This chick calls to the door, roysh, and I can see through the glass that she's actually pretty fit, so when I open the door, I'm like, 'Well, hello there.' Probably a bit sleazy, but fock it. I have to say I'm looking pretty well at the moment and I can actually see her checking me out. I'm there, 'If it's about that catalogue that came through the letterbox during the week, I'm still making my mind up on which purchases to make. Perhaps you'd like to come in for a coffee to discuss it?' She looks at me like I've got ten focking heads. She's very cute. She goes, 'I'm calling about the election.' I'm there, 'What election?' She goes, 'The general election. At the end of May. Have you decided which way you're going to vote?'

What a focking turn-off. I'm just like, 'I don't vote,' and she looks at me real, like, disappointed. She looks a little bit like Kirsten Dunst actually. She goes, 'Apathy is a terrible thing.' I'm like, 'You're wasting your breath. I don't even know what that word means and I don't care either.' She goes, 'What if everybody took your attitude?' I'm like, 'Everyone does. Voting's for old dears. I don't know anyone my age who votes.' She goes, 'Oh right, so you don't care about the kind of country you live in?' I'm like, 'The only thing I care about right now is how I'm going to get the vodka and cranberry juice stain off my beige chinos and how I'm going to get your phone number without having to listen to any more of your boring politics shit.' I was pretty pleased with that. She wasn't. Off she storms up the path, roysh. Her loss.

I shut the door, roysh, and the old man's standing right behind me and he gives me the focking fright of my life. He goes, 'Well said, Kicker. Well said.' I'm like, 'Shut up, Dick-head.' He ignores this. He goes, 'I can feel it, Ross. I can feel it.' I'm there, 'What are you bullshitting on about?' He goes, 'The elbow in my ribs. Hint, hint. You wanted me to run in this elec-tion, didn't you?' I'm like, 'You are *such* a knob.' He goes, 'Oh, I considered it alright. Considered it for the sake of people like you. You and all these other non-voters who are disillusioned with politics. Disillusioned with a capital D. Hennessy thinks I'm the one to capture the youth vote.' I'm like, 'Yeah, roysh. Get real,' and I head into the kitchen. He follows me and he's there going, 'I had policies, make no mistake about that. I had policies coming out of my ears. I'd have had no problem prop-ping up a minority Fianna Fáil administration either, but it would have cost Bertie. An end to all this nonsense about rugby at Knacker Park for starters, a *clear* statement from the Govern-ment that Funderland is an eyesore and an evil that is eating away at the fabric of society in Ballsbridge and Sandymount, as well as a total ban on the sale of batch bread on the southside of Dublin.' I'm like, 'What the fock is batch bread?' He goes, 'Something that poor people eat.' I'm like, 'Well, I've never heard of it.' He goes, 'Of course you haven't. That's why I've been working so hard all these years, Ross. To keep you from it. How do you think all this bloody tribunal nonsense started?' I'm like, 'Look, you're totally boring me now. I'm going out.'

✱ ✱ ✱

I bump into Amy coming out of French Connection. She air-kisses me and asks me if I heard that her old man got her membership for Riverview for her twenty-first and I resist the temptation to go, 'And this affects me how?' and instead I just go, 'Cool.' And she goes, 'OH! MY! GOD! Faye is, like, TOTALLY jealous.' I ask her if she's, like, coming to my twenty-first next week, roysh, and she goes, 'Definitely.' Then she says she has to go because she has a sunbed session booked for, like, three o'clock.

✱ ✱ ✱

'What do you want for your birthday?' That's all anybody's been asking me for the last, like, three weeks, roysh, and I told everyone the same thing. I was like, 'Bianca Luyckx.' Birthday came and guess what? No Bianca Luyckx, same as focking last year. No cord from Sorcha either. I know she's in Australia, but it wouldn't have killed her to send me one. I did have this big, fock-off marquee in the garden and, like, twenty kegs of Ken for my porty. The theme was, like, Rappers and Slappers, roysh. All of the blokes came as either Eminem or P Diddy, and all of the birds came as, like, hookers. Except Erika, roysh, who wouldn't lower herself. She arrives wearing a pair of Karen Millen beige suedette trousers, roysh, and an Amanda Wakeley mesh top with, like, gold and bronze sequins, both of which she's apparently borrowed from Claire. None of us could understand why she was borrowing clothes from her. I mean she could basically buy threads like that with her pocket money and still have enough left over to buy half of focking Nine West. Claire goes up to her about, like, ten minutes into the night and she goes, '*Hello*? You were supposed to dress up as a slapper. You've just put on my clothes.' And Erika just, like, smiles at her, roysh, and Claire's jaw just, like, hits the floor. Erika goes, 'The penny drops.' So a few of the birds had to drag Claire off to the jacks to calm her down, which sort of, like, suited me, roysh, because me and the goys had decided that tonight was a night for, like, serious drinking and we didn't want to be bothered with that whole chatting up birds thing, not until the end of the night anyway.

So there we were knocking back the pints, roysh, and we'd basically come to the part of the night, roysh, when the mince pies and the toilet rolls usually come out, when all of a sudden, roysh, who walks in only my old man with a couple of his mates from the golf club, we're talking Hennessy Coghlan-O'Hara, that asshole of a solicitor of his, and a few others. I'm just like, 'Sorry, what the *fock* are you doing here?' The old man's, like, speechless. He goes, 'Just, em, wanted to pop in, see how you were, er, getting on. See if there's not too much, em … damage.' And then he storts, like, laughing, trying to be my best friend again. I'm like, 'This is *my* focking porty. I don't remember saying you and your dickhead mates were invited.' He's about to answer me, roysh, when all of a sudden I notice the old dear coming in with, like, loads of her mates. I'm like, 'Oh, *great!* The whole focking world's invited.'

The old dear goes, 'Ross, we're just bringing in some food for you and your friends.' And all of a sudden, roysh, they stort putting out all these plates of, like, goats cheese and spinach roulade, crabmeat wrapped in filo pastry, roast vegetable tartlets and whatever. I'm there, '*Hello?* None of this shit, like, goes with beer.'

JP, roysh, he comes over and, like, puts his arm around my old dear and he goes, 'Mrs O'Carroll-Kelly. Looking pretty fine, it *has* to be said.' He looks at me as he says this and, like, raises one eyebrow, the sleazy focker. He looks more like a pimp than a rapper in the tux he wore to the debs, his old dear's fur coat and his old man's trilby. But he's focking loving my embarrassment. Then Oisinn decides to get in on the act. He comes over and he's like, 'Hey, JP, let's bring some happiness into the lives of these beautiful young ladies,' and the lads link arms with the old dear and her friends and head off towards the bor. I think I'm going to basically borf.

I find a quiet corner and stort, like, knocking the beers back, listening to Christian, who's chatting up this complete focking stunner. We're talking Dani Behr-gorgeous here. I don't know who invited her, but I'd like to shake the goy's hand. Christian's explaining to her how the Clone Wars turned Boba Fett into a mercenary soldier, an assassin and the best damn bounty hunter in the Galaxy and that if she ever has any doubt about that fact then she should consider the record 500,000 credits he earned for catching the Ffib religious heretic Nivek'Yppiks for the Lorahns. And this bird, roysh, she's actually totally into it, she goes, 'They should send that goy after Osama bin Laden.' And Christian goes, 'Everybody thinks he's dead. They think the Sarlaac got him, in the Pit of Carkoon. You think the Sarlaac could bite through Mandalorian armour? Oh sure he was injured, but he survived. Dengar found him, when he went back to look for Jabba the Hutt's remains.' The next time I look around, roysh, the two of them are, like, bet into each other.

I turn away and stort wondering whether someone's going to organise the whole twenty-one kisses thing before I'm, like, too off my face to enjoy it. Then this bird comes over, roysh, Danielle's her name, or Measles as the goys call her, basically because everyone's had her once and nobody really wants her a second time. Anyway, she storts, like, boring the ear off me about some goy I've never even heard of who apparently has *such* a commitment problem that he's *never* going to be happy with, like, anyone, and we're talking *anyone*.

I end up knocking over my pint accidentally on purpose just to get away from the psycho bitch and I head back up to the bor, where the old man is locked and shouting his mouth off about rugby. He's there going, 'Doesn't matter what score we lost by to England and France, we're heading in the right direction.' And JP and Oisinn are, like, lapping this up, really egging him on, determined to humiliate me tonight. JP's there going, 'Eddie's the man, eh Charles?' And the old man's like, 'Eddie's the man alright. I'm with Hooky on this one.' I'm just there, 'You said last year that Warren was the man,' which doesn't throw him one little bit. He goes, 'Warren Gatland, my eye! Eddie was always the brains behind the team. And I can tell you that a certain G Thornley of D'Olier Street, Dublin 2, will be eating his words before too long, thank you very much.' And Oisinn, roysh, he's really storting to take the piss now, he goes, 'Why don't you give Gerry a ring?' And for one second, I can see the idea flash across the old man's face because he turns around to see if the old dear's listening. Then he thinks better of it. He goes, 'No, he's changed his number.' I'm like, 'Are you focking surprised?' He goes, 'Do you know how many years I've been buying *The Irish Times*, Ross? Readers are entitled to their opinions.' And I'm like, 'And he was entitled to blow that pest whistle down the phone.' He turns around to Hennessy and he's like, 'I couldn't hear anything for about a week, you know.'

The goys are all lapping this up and I'm pretty much beginning to lose the will to live at this stage. But then suddenly, roysh, it's time for business. A chair is dragged out into the middle of the floor and I'm told to, like, sit on it and all of a sudden Christian stands up and makes this speech about what an amazing hit I am with the chicks, which is true; what an amazing rugby player I am, which is half-true; and what an amazing friend I am, which is total bullshit. When he finishes, roysh, I just high-five the goy and tell him I don't deserve him. He tells me to shut the fock up and sit down and then he goes, 'Okay, ladies, you want to kiss the Corellian, form an orderly queue. If you can control yourselves, that is.'

First up is Danielle. A bit too John B for my liking. She basically tries to have sex with me. Second is Amie, the make-up monster, still mad into me, trying not to show it in front of her boyfriend, but the suit is definitely going to need a dry-clean now. Then it's, like, Zoey, third year commerce with German in UCD, a bit like Mena Suvari and the first tongue of the night. Number four is Claire, as in Dalkey-wannabe Claire, mascara all over her face after her row with Erika, it's like being kissed by a focking Saint Bernard. Number five is Oisinn taking the piss. Next up is Georgia, my ex who used to do the weather on RTÉ, puts the 'boiler' in the word bunnyboiler. Seven is Frederika, JP's ex, second year Russian and Byzantine Studies in UCD, a bit like Charlize Theron. JP's still mad into her, so I pull her onto my knee and make it a big, long one, just to, like, get back at the focker for earlier.

But I don't really enjoy it, roysh, because I can hear Emer and Sophie, numbers eight and nine, talking about how much weight Sorcha has lost since she went to, like, Australia, that's if the photographs are anything to go by. Kissing Emer is like kissing a mate, no fun. Sophie puts both hands around the back of my head, roysh, and gives me what we usually call an 'Ibiza Uncovered' kiss. Then, without batting an eyelid, roysh, she just, like, slips back into her conversation with Emer and she asks her whether there's any points in, like, toothpaste.

Ten is Erika. Sensual is the only way to describe it. When she's finished, she stays sitting on my lap and goes, 'You've wanted that for ages, haven't you?' and I'm sitting there like a focking nodding dog. She goes, 'Happy Birthday,' and I'm so flustered, roysh, that I can't remember eleven, twelve, thirteen and fourteen, but video evidence later confirms them as Melanie, as in Institute Melanie, Ana with one n, Sara with no h and Jessica with no tits. Fifteen is JP ripping the piss. Sixteen is Danielle again. Somebody call security!

Seventeen is this bird Neasa, a Whore on the Shore who gave me, like, a peck on the cheek after we won the Schools Cup and then told all her friends she had been with me. Mind you, I told all mine that I shagged her. Eighteen is this bird, a real BOBFOC job – Body Off 'Baywatch', Face Off 'Crimewatch' – don't know her name and don't want to, she kisses me like she's kissing a focking corpse. Nineteen is Christian's new squeeze, whose name is Lauren and who, it turns out, is Hennessy's daughter, and I wonder how an ugly focker like him could produce something as beautiful as her. I'm still thinking about it while I'm kissing Chloe, number twenty, who gives me two pecks on the lips and, in between, mentions totally out of the blue that the leather coat she's wearing tonight is a Prada and cost, like, two grand, and it dawns on me that after twenty-one years on this Earth I know some totally focked-up people.

I'm wondering what the story is with the twenty-first kiss. Who's it going to be? I see Danielle thinking about it – whoah, horsey! – but Fionn manages to, like, shepherd her into a corner. And then Aoife steps forward, roysh, and I'm thinking, 'Aoife? Sorcha's best mate? This is going to be like kissing, I don't know, my sister, if I had one.' But all of a sudden, roysh, she pulls out this photograph of, like, Sorcha, and slaps it on my lips and she goes, 'She's sorry she couldn't be here to give it to you in person, Ross. I've got a cord for you from her as well.'

And everyone is just, like, clapping, going mental. She probably ripped the idea off one of those stupid American programmes she watches, but basically I couldn't have been happier, even if they had got me Bianca Luyckx.

CHAPTER THREE
The One Where Ross Gets A Babe Lair

In the Stephen's Green Shopping Centre, roysh, I'm on the escalator, coming down from the cor pork and this bird is on the next escalator, on her way up. She's a focking cracker, roysh, a little bit like Uma Thurman up close, and she's with this complete dickhead, a real focking skateboard geek, long-sleeved Nirvana T-shirt, the whole lot, and as our two escalators are passing, roysh, I catch her eye and she's, like, looking straight at me for, like, five seconds and she sort of, like, smiles. And the goy, roysh, he cops this because when we've passed each other, out of the corner of my eye, I can see him looking back, totally paranoid now.

***

The old man, roysh, it's like he's on focking speed half the time. I go into the kitchen the other morning, hanging from the night before, and we're pretty much talking TOTALLY here, and he's like, 'Ross, there you are. Your mother and I bought that CD, the one with the poor people telling stories from the Bible. It's all dis, dat, dees and dose. Cheered your mother right up, it has.' I'm just like, 'When are you two going to focking cop yourselves

on?' and I go back up to my room, SO not in the mood for them
after last night.

It storted off bad, roysh, got good around midnight, then
went, like, downhill after that. It was the usual crack in the M1,
the goys talking about 'Jackass' and the birds tearing the back
off whoever was stupid enough to go to the toilet on their
own. Sophie asks me how my old dear is, roysh, and I say I
don't give a shit, that the bitch deserved what she got, and
Aoife asks what happened, roysh, and Sophie tells her that
some lunatic threw a tin of red paint over my old dear coming
out of that fur shop on Grafton Street. Aoife goes, 'Oh my
God. That is like, OH! MY! GOD!' and Sophie goes, 'TOTALLY.
It is, like, SO not a cool thing to do. It happened to, like, my
mom, too. Except it was, like, blue paint. Mom just looked at
them and she was like, "That will achieve nothing. It is not going to bring the seal back and my husband will just buy me another coat".' Aoife goes, '*Go* Sophie's mom! That is, like,
Hello?' and Sophie goes, 'I know. It SO is.'

It's my round, roysh, so I hit the bor and that's when for one,
like, brief moment the evening storts looking up. Which actually
happens to be my opening line to this stunner I'm standing next
to, a ringer for Tamzin Outhwaite. I'm like, 'The evening is
storting to look up.' She goes, 'That is *such* a bad chat-up line.
You're Ross O'Carroll-Kelly, aren't you?' I'm like, 'The one and
only.' She goes, 'You were with my best friend. Auveen. You
were a bastard to her.' I'm like, 'Doesn't sound like me. Is she the
bird who gave me the Denis on my neck? Hey, I had to shell out
twenty notes for a focking tetanus.' She goes, 'I don't care actually that you were a shit to her. She might be my best friend but
she's an asshole.'

We're getting on really well, roysh, so I drop the drinks over to the lads and I'm like, 'See you goys later,' and Aoife goes, 'Don't tell me you're actually going to *be* with that girl?' I'm there, 'If she plays her cards right … maybe.' Aoife goes, 'Ross, she's been going out with Brad for the last, like, five years. Brad as in Terenure Brad. Brad as in used to be on the Senior Cup team Brad?' Fionn, roysh, the focking crawler, he goes, 'Aoife's right, Ross,' and he pushes his glasses up on his nose. He's there, 'Brad and her are always splitting up. She probably caught him with one of her friends. She wants to get back with him and she's using you as a chip to renegotiate terms.' I'm just like, 'Don't wait up,' which I have to say, roysh, I was pretty pleased with.

To tell you the truth I wasn't actually that Terry Keane on this bird, roysh, but the fact that her boyfriend was Gick made it a challenge I couldn't resist. I go back to the bor, roysh, buy her a Bacardi Breezer, fill her head with a whole load of bullshit about how I've been into her for ages, get a six-pack from the machine in the jacks and the next thing I know, Bob's your auntie's husband, we're in a Jo Maxi on the way to her pad in Leopardstown. I have to say, roysh, I'm really in the mood at this stage, but she turns out to be one of those birds – you know the kind – who wants to watch *Ghost* and *The Piano* and every focking chick flick she owns on video before doing anything, to make the evening, like, romantic or memorable or some shit. But halfway through *You've Got Mail*, I make my move, roysh, and the next thing you know, we're in her bedroom, blah blah blah.

But she keeps saying to me, roysh, 'Say my name, Ross. Say my name,' and that's when I realise, roysh, that I don't know it. So I jump up and I'm like, 'I have to go to the jacks,' and she's like, 'What?' I'm there, 'Sorry, I have to go to the toilet. Back in a second.' She goes, 'Hurry back.' I go into the sitting room, roysh, and stort turning the place over looking for an ESB bill, a TV licence, a framed diploma from, I don't know, LSB, anything with her focking name on it, but I can't find anything. If I go back in there and tell her I don't know it, roysh, I am so out of here it's not funny. So I've, like, no other choice, roysh. I have to go to her handbag, which is on the table in the kitchen. But as I go to pick it up, roysh, I accidentally knock over this load of washing that's hung on the back of one of the chairs. I've got to be quick at this stage, so I stort picking it up with one hand and going through her bag with the other, looking for a student ID, or a driving licence, or anything.

And suddenly, roysh, I can, like, sense that I'm being watched and I sort of, like, stop and I hear her going, 'What the *fock* are you doing?' I turn around and I'm like, 'This isn't … em …' She goes, 'Are you stealing money from me?' I'm like, 'No, I was–' She goes, '*What* were you looking for in my bag?' And I don't know why, roysh, I just said, like, the first thing that came into my head. I was like, 'Lipstick.'

She looks at me, roysh, as though she's, like, weighing this up in her mind, and then she looks down at my hand and, like, her expression suddenly changes. And then I look down and I realise that I'm holding a pair of her tights, and she's staring at me like I'm some kind of weirdo and she goes, 'Lipstick? OH! MY! GOD! You are one sick boy,' I'm like, 'I swear, I'm not one of those trans-whatever you call them.' She opens the door and goes, 'Get out of my apartment! NOW!' I'm like, 'Please don't tell any of the Nure goys about this.' She goes, 'Oh my God, I am SO going to tell *everyone* what a weirdo you are.'

I walk back to my gaff, knowing that by next weekend this'll be all over town. And they'll come up with a focking nickname for me. It'll be Cross O'Carroll-Kelly, how much do you bet?

✱ ✱ ✱

Michelle from Ulster Bank has left another message. She says it's urgent.

✱ ✱ ✱

Asked the old man for two hundred lids. Wanted to get, like, a pair of trousers and a shirt, roysh, and he goes, 'Don't have that kind of money on me, Ross. But your mother and I are going into the city this afternoon. You can get whatever you want on my card.' I'm like, 'Which means I'm going to have to go into town with you two?' He goes, 'Yes, what's the problem, Kicker? Lovely summer's day ...' And I go, 'Do you *honestly* think I want to spend my day hanging out with you knobs.'

Basically I'd no other choice, though. I was going to Annabel's that night, pretty much guaranteed my bit off Ali, this bird who's, like, first year morkeshing in Mountjoy Square, and I needed new threads. So I lash on the old fleece, collar up, and my baseball cap – pulled down over my eyes obviously – and get into the back of the old man's cor, bricking it in case anyone, like, recognises me. We pork the cor in the Arnott's cor pork, focking northside, and head towards Grafton Street. The old man looks a total dickhead as per usual in his camel-hair coat and that stupid focking hat he wears. The old dear has the usual fifty baby seals on her back and I'm just there, 'Oh my God, I SO have to get away from these two.' The old man's like, 'Slow down, Kicker,' but I'm walking, like, fifty metres ahead of them and the one time I do look back, roysh, is when I'm halfway up Grafton Street and the two of them are looking in the window of Weirs, her hanging off his arm, obviously trying to get another piece of Lladro out of the focker.

So I head on into BT2, roysh – they know where to find me – and I hit the old Hugo Boss section first and stort thinking about getting a new pair of loafers. My old ones are, like, a bit scuffed. The next thing, roysh, who do I bump into only Jill, this mate of Ali's, roysh, who does a bit of modelling and she goes, 'Oh my God, *hi*,' and sort of, like, air-kisses me. I'm like, 'Hey, babes, how goes it?' flirting my orse off with her. She's there, 'Oh my God, Ali's just, like, texted me this second. Are you going to, like, Annabel's tonight?' I'm like, 'I could find myself in that vicinity,' playing it totally Kool and the Gang.

Anyway, roysh, all of this is sort of, like, by the by, because what happened next was I suddenly heard all this, like, shouting and shit over by the escalators, and I recognise the old man's voice and I turn around, roysh, and there he is, arguing with these two coppers who, like, have a hold of him. He's there going, 'You are not arresting us. We have *rights*.' And the old dear's going, 'Do you even *know* who we are?' I presumed it had something to do with the tribunal. Of course, they stort trying to drag me into it then. The old man spots me and he's straight over, going, 'Ross, phone Hennessy. Tell him what's happened,' making a total show of me in front of Jill and half of focking Grafton Street. I just look at him, roysh, and I'm like, 'Sorry, have we met before?' He goes, 'Ross, phone Hennessy. Tell him–' and the next thing the cops drag him and the old dear off and Jill's there going, 'OH! MY! GOD! that is, like, SO embarrassing. Who *were* those people?' I'm like, 'I don't know.' Jill goes, 'They seemed to know you. The man called you Ross.' I'm like, 'Probably recognised me from the papers. I get that all the time.' She goes, 'Oh my God, yeah, you play rugby,' and then she's like, 'My dad went to that game against England when we lost? They must have been SO down afterwards. I said it to Ali. I was like, "Oh my God, I would SO love to give them all a hug",' which is when I realised, roysh, what a total sap Jill was and I decided to push on.

The only downside of the old pair being arrested, roysh, was that I couldn't get my new threads and also that I had to get, like, the bus home. I thought my public transport days were well and truly behind me, but there I am, roysh, upstairs on the 46a, texting JP and Christian to find out what the Jackanory is about tonight, when all of a sudden my mobile rings and it's, like, the old man. He's like, 'Ross, do *not* panic. We're being held in Harcourt Terrace. Now, have you phoned Hennessy?' I'm like, 'Phone him yourself.' He goes, 'Okay, let's stay calm. We've got to think carefully. That's mandatory. Now, I'm only allowed one phone call and I've called you.' I'm like, 'Bad call then.' He's there, 'Hennessy's in Jersey, Ross. He's staying at that new golf resort I told him about. The number's in my Filofax. In the study. Hurry, Ross. Before your mother's coat gets infested.'

I'm like, 'I'm not phoning him. I'm too busy for this shit.' He goes, 'Ross, please. You should see some of the things that are written on the walls in here.' I'm like, 'Why the fock are you ringing Hennessy? He's the goy who said you wouldn't spend a single afternoon in jail.' He goes, 'What? Oh, this has nothing to do with that tribunal nonsense, Ross. We were arrested for jaywalking.' And I just, like, broke my shite laughing, roysh, for about, like, five minutes. Everyone on the bus was looking at me, going, 'Oh my God, what is the story?' The old man's like, 'You know those lights at the bottom of Grafton Street, they take a bloody age to change. So we just crossed, and some bloody garda comes chasing after us and catches up with us at Weir's. Now phone Hennessy. I'm planning to take an action against the State for this.'

I'm like, 'Do you remember that time when I got arrested during the summer? In Martha's Vineyard? What did you say?' He goes, 'Ross, I can hear your mother sobbing in the cell next door.' I'm like, 'You told me you'd decided to let me stew. To teach me a lesson.' I can hear him, like, banging on the door of his cell, going, 'LET US OUT OF HERE. ARE WE LIVING IN CHILE ALL OF A SUDDEN?' I'm there, 'So now it's payback time. I hope you like prison food,' and then I just, like, hang up on the dickhead.

Of course, half-eight, roysh, I'm getting ready to go out when the old pair arrive back at the gaff looking pretty wrecked. The old dear takes to the bed straight away. I turn to the old man and I'm like, 'Well, Nelson, how does it feel to finally be free?' He gives me this filthy, roysh, and he goes, 'You think this is a joking matter?' I'm like, 'You're lucky I can see the funny side of it. You made a total show of me in BT2.' He goes, 'I have only one thing I want to say to you, Ross. I want you to find somewhere else to live. Your mother and I are tired of your unpleasantness, frankly. We think it's time you stood on your own two feet in life. And we want you out of the house by the end of next week.'

I'm like, 'Fock.'

*** * ***

I'm in Reynards, roysh, and I'm with this bird, Helena I think her name is. I sort of, like, know her to see from the rugby club, not bad looking, a little bit like Thora Birch but with less eye make-up. Anyway, there we are, roysh, basically wearing the face off one another and I come up for air, roysh, and she looks at me and goes, 'Oh my God, I have fancied you for SO long.' I'm like, 'I've fancied you for ages too.' I couldn't swear blind that her name is Helena. She goes, 'OH! MY! GOD! you are going to think this is SO sad, but a couple of years ago, you got off the Dart in, like, Killiney, and I was walking just behind you, and you left your ticket on, like, the turnstile thing. And I picked it up. It's been in my wallet for, like, two years. Will I show you?' I stort, like, edging away from her. She goes, 'Oh my God, you probably think I am *such* a weirdo, do you?' Nope, I think you're a focking psycho. I'm like, 'No, no, I'm just going to get us another bottle of wine.' She picks up the bottle on the table and goes, 'But we're not even halfway through this one.' I'm like, 'I just want to see if they've got anything dearer.' I head for the cloakroom, grab my jacket, get the Fightlink home.

✱ ✱ ✱

It turns out the old pair were serious about focking me out of the gaff, roysh, unless I apologised for what happened. *As if.* Packed my rucksack and opened the front door and the old man comes out of the sitting room, roysh, big sad face on the focker, and he goes, 'We could put this behind us, Ross. All you have to do is say you're sorry.' I'm like, 'Yeah, roysh. Get real.' Of course the old dear comes out then, playing the whole concerned parent bit, going, 'Ross, where are you going to stay?' I'm like, 'I don't think that's any of your business anymore, do you? Take a good, long look at me, both of you. It's the last time you'll ever see me.'

I could hear the old dear bawling her eyes out, roysh, and I kind of regretted saying that last bit because I was still hoping the old man would give me the money for my cor insurance, which is up, like, next month. Of course he probably won't even pay it now, that's the kind of dickhead he is. Anyway, roysh, the reason I was able to be so, like, Jack the Lad about being focked out was that I already had somewhere else to stay. Fionn's old pair had bought him an apartment in Dalkey for his twenty-first and basically I was going to be, like, kipping on his sofa for the foreseeable future. But I needed funds, so I had to, like, get a job, which meant dropping out of college, though I didn't mind that so much because I'm pretty sure I failed all my summer exams again and the idea of having to do first year a third time was SO wrecking my head, and we're talking TOTALLY here.

Basically I had a job lined up pretty much straight away. I'd had a few scoops the night before with JP, who's doing an MDB, we're talking Managing Daddy's Business, namely Hook, Lyon and Sinker Estate Agents. When he floated the idea of working with him, I was like, 'JP, I'd literally do anything. Well, within reason. I'm not photocopying, or answering phones, or shit. I don't want anyone taking focking liberties. But I need lids, man. I'm desperate.' He goes, 'Ten-four, Ross. I'm hearing you. Let's fast-track this idea.' JP speaks fluent morkeshing. I'm like, 'What I want is to stort on Monday morning.' He goes, 'I'll talk to the old man tomorrow. See if he'll take the idea off-line. I'll touch base with you in the afternoon.' So JP texts me the next day, roysh, tells me his old man thought it was a win-win situation, which basically means I got the job.

Monday morning I'm out of the scratcher really early, we're talking half-eight here, and I head into the office in Donnybrook, big focking plush gaff, really handy for Kiely's. JP high-fives me and gives me a list of, like, definitions that I have to basically learn off by heart. It's, like, a whole new language and shit. It's all, 'Innovative use of space – pokey as fock. High specification

fit-out kitchen – cooker and fridge. Tranquil waterfront setting – overlooking the Dargle. Parkland setting – grass verge nearby (for now). Dublin 24 – Tallafornia.'

I've just finished reading it when JP's old man arrives, big dog-turd of a cigar clamped between his teeth, a complete focking sleazebag, and he goes, 'Have you told him about the T-word, JP?' I'm like, 'You mean Tallaght?' and he slams his briefcase down on my desk and goes, 'That's the first and last time you ever say that word in this office. *Capisce*?' I'm like, 'Eh, yeah. Kool and the Gang.' He goes, 'Don't ever use that word. It's Dublin 24. Blessington if you're really feeling cocky. But *never* what you just said. Office rules numbers one, two and three.' He storts, like, examining the end of his cigar, which has gone out, and he's there, 'There's worse places, of course. Some of the areas we sell houses in, Christ, you should see them. The queues outside the post office on family allowance day. Like Poland twenty years ago.' He turns around all of a sudden, roysh, points at JP and goes, 'What do we love?' and JP, roysh, quick as a flash, goes, 'The free market,' and his old man goes, 'Yes, we do. Yes, we do. Sorry, Ross. Little game we play.'

He lights his cigar again, takes a few short drags on it and goes, 'I'm going to level with you, kid. We sell a lot of houses here and most of them – honestly? – I wouldn't expect our dog to stay in them. AND I DON'T EVEN LIKE OUR DOG. It was the wife who wanted it. Had a cute face, you see. Two more words we don't use, Ross – at least not in this exact juxtaposition – are NEGATIVE and EQUITY. It's the time to buy. Tell them that. TIME TO BUY! Every house you're selling, you say, "Strong capital appreciation predicted," and say it in great, big capital letters. STRONG CAPITAL APPRECIATION PREDICTED!' JP hands me a cup of coffee and goes, 'Welcome to the firm, Ross,' and his old man goes, 'Your father, does he still own those two apartments in Seapoint? Might give him a call. Really is the time to sell, you know.'

✳ ✳ ✳

I don't know why they call it Boomerangs. I said that to the bouncer who focked me out on Wednesday night. I was like, 'I don't know why they call it Boomerangs. I won't be coming back.'

✳ ✳ ✳

JP's old man says he wants to interface with me Friday a.m., which basically means he wants to talk to me on Friday morning, roysh, to find out how I'm getting on with the two or three pages of estate agent vocab he gave me to, like, learn off and shit. He goes, 'No wall, no fence?' and I'm like, 'Open-plan front garden.' He's like, 'Two plug sockets in every room?' and I go, 'Generous electrical specification.' He goes, 'Ballymun?' and I'm like, 'Glasnevin.' Then he sort of, like, squints his eyes, roysh, and he goes, 'I don't usually rush these things, Ross, but I think you're ready to start selling.' I'm like, 'Well, I know I'm not even here a week yet, but I feel I'm ready too.' He goes, 'Tell you what, let's get a couple of grande frappuccinos to celebrate. Better make them skinny milk, decaf, cinnamon, no chocolate. This bloody heart of mine. Better start listening to the doctor. I pay him enough.'

He calls in his secretary, roysh, quite a good-looking bird I have to say, but CHV – we're talking TOTAL Council House Vermin here – and he sends her out to the shop, his eyes sort of, like, looking her up and down as she goes out the door. He goes, 'Was that a ladder in her tights or a stairway to heaven?' and I break my shite laughing, roysh, even though hearing him say it makes me feel sort of, like, sick.

He sits back in his chair then, lights his cigar and goes, 'Ross, what do you know about the M50?' I'm like, 'Is it, like, a road?' He goes, 'Of a kind, yes. It's a motorway.' I'm there, 'Where does it go?' He's like, 'Who knows, Ross? Who knows?' and he goes into a trance for a few seconds. I'm like, 'Are you okay, Mr Conroy?' He goes, 'Oh sorry, Ross. The M50, yes. I don't even think the focking thing's finished yet. Doesn't matter. Not from our POV anyway. The point is this: people think this motorway is the solution to all life's problems, a superhighway to eternal happiness, if you like. No matter where you're selling a house, kid, you tell 'em it's close to the M50, offering convenient access to, I don't know, the Pampas, Lake Victoria and the focking Hanging Gardens of Babylon … hey, I might put that into some of our prospectuses.'

I'm just, like, nodding, pretending I agree with the goy. I need the shekels. He's like, 'The other matter I need to discuss with you is this,' and he hands me this photograph, roysh, and I'm there, 'What the fock …' He goes, 'Pretty, isn't it?' I'm like, 'Y-y-yeah.' He goes, 'It's called the Luas.' I'm like, 'It … looks like a spaceship.' He's there, 'Well, we'll probably all have spaceships by the time that thing sees the light of day. But mention it, Ross. "Convenient to Luas line." No matter where the house is.

'Amenities, too. People *love* amenities. Ham them up. Within walking distance of shops. And theatres. Bung that in. Restaurants. Of course they won't be able to afford to eat in the restaurants when they're mortgaged up to their town halls, but we deal in dreams here, Ross. People's dreams. WHAT DO WE DEAL IN?' and I automatically go, 'People's dreams,' feeling like a total knob-end, and we're talking big-time total here.

He's like, 'Within walking distance. A key phrase, Ross. Within walking distance. Pretty soon you'll find those words tripping off your tongue. I describe every house we sell as being within walking distance of the city centre. Donnybrook. Clontarf. Dun Laoghaire. Sold one in Balbriggan a couple of weeks ago. Within walking distance of O'Connell Street, I said. Have you ever heard of the Jarrow Marchers, Ross?' I'm like, 'Em … are they in the Super-12?' He goes, 'No, they were a group of workers who … did you do history at school?' I'm like, 'Well, yeah, but I was on the S.' He goes, 'Of course you were.'

He storts, like, rooting around in his drawer then, roysh, and he pulls out another picture and hands it to me and it's of this gaff, roysh, a really shitty-looking place which he says is down some really dark alleyway off, like, Sheriff Street. And he goes, 'A focking mugger's paradise. Two bedrooms. No garden. Every piece of wood in the house crawling with worms. You're looking for three hundred thou for this baby. Well?' I'm like, 'Em …' He goes, 'What do you say to me?' I'm like, 'It's, em … it's, em …' He's there, 'Sell it to me, Ross. SELL IT TO ME!' And I sort of, like, blurt out, 'It's an oasis in the heart of one of the city's more mature areas.' And he just, like, stares at me for ages, roysh, like he's in total shock, then he gets up from his desk and storts, like, staring out the window. I'm like, *Hello?* What the fock is going down here? And it's only then, roysh, that I cop the fact that he's actually crying. He's, like, bawling his focking eyes out. I'm there, 'Hey, man, what's wrong?' and he turns around, roysh, and he's got tears, like, streaming down his face and he goes, 'I wish you were my son.'

✱ ✱ ✱

People have basically been surprised at the state of the gaff me and Fionn are living in. There's, like, no beer cans lying around the place, no, like, Chinese takeaway cartons, no funny smells and even the toilet is, like, flushable. The place is pretty much like a museum, roysh, not because of anything me and Fionn have done – who will ever forget the state of our gaff in Ocean City? – but because of Nicola, this Bulgarian bird who Fionn's old dear pays to come and, like, clean up after us three days a week. She's not the Mae West lookswise – a little bit David Duchovny except with a moustache – but you have to give it to her, roysh, she's a dab hand with a duster and a cloth, and if I were an ordinary goy with simpler needs, I could see me and Nicola getting it on.

The only thing she won't do, roysh, apart from electrolysis, is iron. We've tried to slip her a few extra shekels but it's, like, no go, she will not do it. After three weeks in the gaff, roysh, every single piece of clothing that me and Fionn owned was basically dirty and we were in BT2 every second or third day, splashing out on new threads because we didn't want to face washing and ironing the other ones. But one night, roysh, there we are watching some shite on the Discovery Channel about the Kodiak bear, with Fionn just, like, absorbing all of the information like a sponge, when all of a sudden, during an ad break, he turns around to me and goes, 'We're going to have to do something about that pile of clothes on the landing.' I'm there, 'What about it?' He's like, 'Ross, there are EU food mountains that are worth less than our stockpile of designer threads. Must be ten grand's worth of dirty clothes up there. And I can't afford to buy any more.' I'm like, 'I am SO not asking my old dear to do it, if that's what you're getting at. Wouldn't give that bitch the pleasure.' He goes, 'No, but this solution does require courage nonetheless. I think you should go to see Daisy.'

Daisy, roysh, she's this bird we both know from Lillies, a bit of a bowler if the truth be told, but she has the total hots for yours truly. She's only human, I suppose. Anyway, roysh, Daisy's a bit, like, mumsy, if you know what I mean, she's basically looking for a goy to mother, and one night, roysh, there we were, sat in the corner of Lillies – her getting all, like, touchy-feely, me basically keeping her at bay with a ten-foot bargepole – and she mentioned that she knew how utterly useless goys were around the house, and if we ever needed anyone to come out and, like, cook or iron or anything like that, then we could give her a shout, not knowing of course that she was, like, talking herself into a little weekend job.

So I give her a bell, roysh, and she says she'd be SO happy to come around and do it for us. I'm like, 'There's quite a lot of it, Daisy. Don't make any plans for Saturday or Sunday.' She goes, 'Well, in future I'll come around every Saturday morning to do it. It won't take any longer than a couple of hours a week, once you don't let it pile up.' There'll be a payback for this, you can be sure of that. I'll be expected to be with her now and I have to say, roysh, without being too dramatic here, I actually feel a bit dirty after I hang up the phone. I head outside to Fionn, roysh, who's in the forecourt, looking under the bonnet of his cor – a black Peugeot 206, 1.1 litre, no alloys. He's had trouble storting it lately. I tell him that Daisy's coming out on Saturday morning and I told her to, like, get here early as well. Fionn goes, 'Do you think she knows anything about carburettors?'

✳ ✳ ✳

I actually thought that Erika was just being a bitch to Claire when she mentioned that she'd spent the weekend in Clonakilty at, like, the hunt ball, which was amazing and – OH! MY! GOD! – SO much better than last year. Everyone knows that she hates her, roysh, what with Claire getting caught one night telling some goy in Lillies that she was 'originally from Dalkey' even though she's actually from Bray, and Erika hates people getting above their station. And then there was the time she, like, picketed the fur shop on Grafton Street with, like, Sorcha, during that whole Save The Animals phase they went through in, like, first year in college.

And Claire, roysh, she is SO going to go for the bait. I'm basically watching her, sipping her vodka and Smirnoff Ice and, like, pretending to be interested in some shite Christian's spouting about George Lucas and his willingness to take even more risks with the second trilogy than he did with the first. But Erika's blabbing on and on about all these, like, really rich goys she met down there, roysh, and Claire basically can't control herself anymore.

She goes, 'Don't tell me you, like, killed an animal?' and Erika sort of, like, looks her up and down, roysh, and goes, 'The dogs actually do the killing, Dear,' knowing full well that Claire hates it when she calls her that. I can see her face going red. It's like she's going to focking burst. And Erika goes, 'It was a fox, if you must know. Or it was before the dogs tore it to pieces.' Of course, Christian's there still banging on about 'the boundless creativity of not just Lucas but everyone who works at Skywalker Ranch,' totally oblivious to what's going down here, and we are talking TOTALLY here.

Claire's not saying anything, roysh, just basically bulling quietly to herself. But Erika's not going to let go. She's like one of those dogs she was going on about, ripping the poor fox apart. She's there going, 'Are you about to stort crying?' and Claire goes, 'No,' but she's lying, roysh, and Erika's like, 'Oh my God, you *are*. The tears are welling up in your eyes. That's so sweet. Crying for dead Mister Fox.'

✳ ✳ ✳

Fionn comes home from college, roysh, and he tells me about this coffee place in town, roysh, and when you gave your order they used to say, 'Is that to take away?' Now they say, 'Is that to go?' I'm like, 'And your point is?'

✳ ✳ ✳

I'm, like, texting JP the other day, roysh, trying to find out what the fock OFCH stands for before I try to sell this couple a gaff in Leixlip, and I end up missing a call, and it's actually news to me, roysh, that you can't, like, get through to me on the phone while I'm texting someone. Then again, roysh, it was the old pair who bought me this heap of shit so it shouldn't be, like, a surprise or anything. Anyway, to cut a long story short, I check my messages and, speak of the devil, it's Dickhead himself. I wondered how long it'd be before they came crawling back to me, begging me to come back home. Losers.

The message is like, 'Hey, Ross, how ya doing, Kicker? Em … it's your old dad here. Don't like talking to these machines. Silly that, I know, in this age of … technology and so forth. Em … I was just ringing to see how you were doing, you know, whether you needed, em, any money or anything. I know your car insurance is due. Don't worry about that. I'll look after it. And any other money you need for clothes and so forth … well, em, I guess what I really wanted to say, Ross, is that we're, em, that is your mother and I, we're worried about you. That's both of us, we're both worried. Basically thought you might have been in touch by now.

'All families have their rows, Ross. I guess the lesson that I myself personally have learned, or rather we've learned, we've all learned, from this is that you shouldn't let these things fester. If you let things fester, then, well, pus starts to be produced and then a sort of, em, well a scab forms, and once you've a scab there, then the only thing that can … sorry, Ross, me wittering on as usual. Stretching the metaphor to breaking point as per usual. With a capital S.

'Look, Ross, we're worried. You haven't been in touch and, em, I hear you've dropped out of college. I don't want to get on your case, start lecturing you, but are you sure that's wise? I mean, it's a diploma in sports management. Could come in very handy if you want a career in, em … well, in sports management, I suppose. Don't hang up, Ross. Okay, I'm nagging again. *Mea culpa. Mea culpa.* Probably wittering again as well. It's these machines. I've never liked … anyway, em, I hear you're working with JP's dad now. In Hook, Lyon and Sinker. Young Christian told us. Your mother and I met him in the Frascati Centre last week. A strange young man, Christian. A bit, I don't know, away with the fairies.

'Hey, I know it was a few months ago now, but me and a couple of the guys got chatting about the Munster versus Castres match in the golf club the other night. A good old-fashioned debate we had on the relative merits and demerits of David Humphries and a certain R O'Gara, Esquire, of Cork, who I know you're a fan of. He did do well in that game, I'll grant you that. But you know where I stand in the great debate, Ross. I'm a Humphries man, always have been. Make no apologies for it, either. David Humphries, record Irish points kicker. But, well, I had to admit it, young O'Gara did give me something to think about in that game. Anyway, there is a point to this. What I was going to tell you was that Hennessy was there and at one point in the conversation I popped the sixty-four-million-dollar question to him. 'Hennessy,' I said, 'you're Eddie O'Sullivan tonight. The choice is Humphries or O'Gara. Shoot!' He looked at me, Ross, wiped his cigar ash onto the side of the ashtray, you know the way he does that, and he said, 'Charles, that lad of yours is a better kicker than the pair of them.' Wasn't that a great thing to hear? He didn't have to say it, Ross, but he did.

'So … it's a career in estate agency then? Em … no, it's a good job. Satisfying, I'd imagine. I hope you're not doing anything too dangerous … selling houses in Tallaght and whatnot. Your mother said that the other night. She said, "He could be any-where, Charles. He could be in Tallaght." You know those night-mares she's been having, Ross. She worries, you see. Maybe give her a call. Both of us. Maybe give us both a call. When you get this message.

'Em … well, I suppose I've gone on long enough. What I guess I'm trying to say is that we're sorry, Ross. We're sorry for telling you to leave the house. You can come home anytime. But, em, really, Ross, please call. Oh, by the way, Michelle from Ulster Bank called. Wants to know can you ring her back. It sounded urgent.'

✳ ✳ ✳

I meet Emer on Grafton Street, coming out of Nine West. I'm like, 'Hey, how's it going, Emer?' She goes, 'Great, I weigh nothing.'

✳ ✳ ✳

Had this, like, dilemma the other day, roysh. JP's old man asked me to show this couple around this gaff in Foxrock. TOTALLY amazing pad, we're talking eight bedrooms, swimming pool, electric gates, big fock-off driveway, we're talking one-and-a-half-million bills and basically a nice little commission for me, roysh, if I can, like, offload the thing. The problem was that it was the gaff next door to my old pair's, and I was SO not in the mood for bumping into those two saps.

I think I've already mentioned, roysh, that my old man is basically a dickhead and my old dear, roysh, is a complete knob, and the last thing I needed in my life at that stage was the two of them telling me how, like, proud they are of me now that I'm working as an estate agent and her going on about how much she misses me and wants me to come home, the sad bitch that she is. I couldn't actually handle the two of them, but like I said, roysh, the commission on this was big, we're basically talking serious sponds here, and not only that, roysh, I SO didn't want to let JP's old man down. Not being, like, big-headed or anything, roysh, but he thinks I'm pretty amazing at the job, which has put JP's nose roysh out of joint, and we're talking big-style.

Last week, roysh, there I was, on the phone, basically trying to bleed an extra five grand out of this bloke for this complete focking dump in East Wall and it was all, 'Well, we might be able to raise the money if we think about sending Joshua to a less upmarket school,' so I got him to pay, like, five grand over the asking price in the end, roysh, and when I put the phone down, JP's old man just looks at me and goes, 'Your heart, Ross, it's just for pumping blood around your body, isn't it?' I just, like, shrug and go, 'Hey, it's business,' and he's, like, SO impressed by that.

Anyway, I drive up outside the gaff next door to the old pair, roysh, and there's this, like, shitty old Nissan Bluebird outside, we're talking a 90D bucket of focking rust here, and it's, like, blocking the entrance to the driveway. Of course, I'm straight on the mobile, roysh, calling the cops, the last thing I need is for the prospective buyers to see that pile of shit and think there's a halting site up the road. But all of a sudden, roysh, I notice there's a bloke sitting in the passenger seat, so I, like, get out and walk up to his window, roysh, and I'm like, 'Would you mind moving that thing?' He's there, 'Sorry, bud?' He's a complete focking howiya, this goy, slip-on shoes, side-parting, newsprint moustache. I'm like, 'I'm supposed to be showing someone around this house in a minute. No offence, roysh, but the last thing I want them to see when they turn up is the likes of you and this little crock of shit.' It shocks me how like my old man I can sound sometimes. He goes, 'Sorry, bud, I think you've got yisser facts wrong. I'm here to luke over the house, so I am. Me and de wife.'

I'm like, 'Roysh, but I think you're the one with your facts wrong. The guide price is one and a half million, not fifteen thousand. You've miscounted the noughts.' 'No, no, no, bud,' he goes, 'we know what the price is. See, we're after winnin' the Lorro.' I was, like, OH! MY! GOD! Erika is right, there should be laws to limit the amount of money that jackpot winners can spend on new houses, to prevent areas like Dalkey and Donnybrook from losing their character. I mean, Foxrock is going to *love* this focker. I actually remember now seeing him in the paper. Four million he basically won.

His wife gets out of the cor then, roysh, and she is total CHV, and we're talking TOTAL here. She goes, 'Are you the fella what's going to show us around?' and I'm thinking about saying something smart, roysh, like asking her husband to translate what she's saying into English, but I don't, roysh, because as we're walking up towards the gate, roysh, I'm thinking of my old man, living on the other side of that fence over there. Oisinn said he saw him in town last Saturday with the old dear, on Grafton Street, with his focking sheepskin coat on, and he was talking to this, like, beggar who asked him if he'd any change to spare for a cup of tea. And the old man was going, 'You asked me the same thing this morning. Seems to me that you drink far too much tea, young chap. Bad for you, all that caffeine. Makes you sluggish. Probably why you've no home and no job.'

So I think about what a sap he is, roysh, and then I think about the shit that this pair, and however many kids they have, are going to make of the area, putting tyres around the lampposts, and whatever. And then I think about JP's old man's last words as I, like, left the office. He goes, 'Remember, you're not only selling a house here, Ross. You're choosing your parents' neighbours,' and he said it with, like, a twinkle in his eyes because he knows I hate my old pair. So as I'm opening the electric gates into the gaff, roysh, I turn around to them and I go, 'You are SO going to love this house. And the good news is, I'm prepared to be flexible on the price.'

✳ ✳ ✳

There's, like, three messages on my phone this morning. One is from Aoife, who was ringing just to wish me good luck with the holiday and to tell all the goys the same. The second is from this bird, Sally, who's heard a rumour that I like to take a trophy when I've been with a girl and all she wants to know – 'I'm SO not pissed off, I just want to *know*' – if that's what happened to her

*NSync *No Strings Attached* album, and *if* it is she'd be really upset because it was, like, a birthday present from her mum. The other is from Michelle from Ulster Bank, who's obviously just noticed that my account is in the black again, basically for the first time since my Confirmation, and she wants to talk to me about an SSIA, whatever the fock that is.

CHAPTER FOUR
The One Where Ross Goes Native

The captain says that unless the music is turned off immediately, the plane won't be going anywhere and we hear this voice down the back shout, 'Careeeena, torn it off, will ye?' And this Carina bird goes, 'It's not my fookin ghetto-blaster, it's Anto's.' And Fionn, roysh, he takes off his glasses, rubs his eyes and goes, 'It's like being trapped in a focking Roddy Doyle novel.' I'm sitting between him and Christian, roysh, and I've already won the battle for elbow room, Fionn putting up a little bit more resistance than I'd expected. JP and Oisinn are sitting in front of us.

The air hostess is up the front of the plane, roysh, giving out the instructions, obvious shit like make sure you take the cigarette out of your mouth before you put your oxygen mask on, otherwise your face will focking explode. Then the bird, roysh, you'd have to feel sorry for her, she puts on the life jacket and all the cream crackers down the back are giving it, 'Very sexy on ye.' And then, roysh, when she's showing us how to inflate the thing, they're all cheering and going, 'You can blow into my tube any time you like.' Oisinn turns around and goes, 'We're going to be turned back before we get there, what's the bet?'

Going on a knacker holiday was JP's idea. 'A little-known

island off the coast of Africa,' was what he told us. Playa del focking Ingles. But JP loves this kind of thing. It makes him feel, like, superior and shit. He's looking over the back of his seat, going, 'Look at all these peasants, Ross. Did you bring johnnies?' I'm like, 'Of course,' and he nods his head and goes, 'We leave nothing to chance, goys. We go out fully dressed. Last thing any of us wants is to be paying child support to one of these slappers for the rest of our lives. I am certainly not giving up half my trust fund for some little focking Natalie.'

No sooner are we in the air, roysh, than the music's back on, full blast. Bob focking Marley. *'Evy little ting gonna be alroy.'* Fionn turns to me, roysh, and he goes, 'You can't deny it's extraordinary, Ross ...' but I'm too busy trying to read this decent-looking air hostess's name badge without her thinking I'm scoping her baps. Fionn goes, 'Are you ignoring me?' I'm like, 'Is this another one of your theories?' He goes, 'Ross, unlike the Institute, I've never charged you for the education I've given you. So be grateful. And keep up. I'm talking about Bob Marley and the universal nature of his music.' I'm like, 'And your point is?' He goes, 'His *métier*, Ross, is misery. Which is why from Trenchtown to Ballyfermot, from Harlem to focking Coolock, his music is the soundtrack to knackers' lives the world over. *That's* my focking point.'

A bird walks by on her way to the jacks, milk-bottle-white arms and legs, butterfly tattoo on her shoulder, every bit of focking jewellery she owns hanging off her. Oisinn puts his head up, sniffs the air and goes, 'Shit the bed, that girl's wearing *Brut.'* Christian's, like, totally quiet, roysh, so I try to get a bit of conversation out of him. I'm there, 'Long old flight, isn't it?' and he looks at me like he's about to deck me and he goes, 'Travelling through hyper-space ain't like dusting crops, boy,' so I just leave him. The next thing I hear, roysh, is some other skanger down the back shouting, 'Byrner, stick on the Tones.' And the CD goes on, roysh, and suddenly it's all, *'Come out you Black and Tans, come and fight me like a man, tell your wife how you won medals down in Flaaaanders.'* And I turn around, roysh, and who's down the back of the plane with them, taking his life into his hands, only JP. Eight pints of Ken in the airport bor and four vodka and tonics on the flight and he's singing away with all the creamers, arms around shoulders, the lot. *'Tell her how the IRA, made you run like fuck away, down the green and leafy lanes of Killeshaaaandra.'* And he keeps, like, pointing up at us, going, 'Sorry about my friends, goys. A bit too stuck-up for the likes of us.'

He's totally ripping the piss out of them. At one point I hear him asking whether anyone has a spare Celtic jersey because he's left his behind. He is SO going to get himself killed it's not funny. So we're, like, majorly relieved when we land and we hang back while this big stampede of skangers heads for, like, the door of the plane, which turns out to be a bit of a mistake, roysh, because by the time we get to, like, passport control, the queues are out the focking door. Oisinn goes, 'This'll take half the night. Half these fockers are only out on temporary release.'

We finally get through, grab our bags and get on the bus. Me and the goys sit up the front, except for JP who's now wearing a green-and-white football shirt that we saw him putting on at the, like, baggage carousel, and he goes down the back with his new mates and storts making arrangements to meet them tomorrow night in some bor or other. One of the skangers is like, 'We're after bein' here this last four year. We know all the good spots.' And JP's like, 'Wonderful,' putting on this really, like, exaggerated posh voice that's going to earn him, like, a punch in the face before we get to our apartment. The blokes are like, 'We can get good blow as well.' JP goes, 'You mean cannabis? *Splendid.*'

So me and the goys are just sitting there, going, 'That goy is SO on his own on this holiday.' But then, roysh, to cap it all, it turns out we're all staying in exactly the same gaff – me and the goys are in with the focking cast of *The Commitments*. And what a focking kip it looked. You should have seen our faces when this great big tower block appeared out of, like, nowhere. Oisinn, roysh, he summed it up best. He's like, 'Shit the bed, it's Bally-mun-on-Sea.'

✱ ✱ ✱

JP's new favourite expression is, 'The Poverty Trap.' He shouts it at the top of his voice everywhere we go – in the middle of the supermarket, having a few scoops out on the balcony, walking along the beach. The other night, roysh, he shouts it in The Irish Jockey. He's up at the bor, getting his round in, roysh, and he puts his arm around this total focking creamer he's never even met before, he sort of, like, turns the goy around to face us and he shouts, 'THE POVERTY TRAP!' A knife will be pulled on him before the holiday is out. Of that you can be basically sure. The Irish Jockey is where you go in Playa del Ingles if you want to, like, listen to Irish music, talk about how many times you'd be prepared to die for Ireland, moan about how the focking Canaries isn't Ireland and then bag off with some slapper from Dublin late enough in the night not to have to buy her a Ritz. The only chat-up line you'll ever need in there is, 'So, what Dorsh station do you work in yourself?' which is basically not my idea of a good night out.

I had a totally different kind of evening planned this particular night, roysh, and we're talking TOTALLY here. I spent the first,

like, three days of the holiday putting in the spadework on these two Spanish birds, roysh, total focking honeys, we're talking Penelope Cruz and focking Shakira here. And there I am, roysh, the first couple of days, giving them the odd wink and smile down by the pool, flashing the pecs when I'm, like, putting on the old factor two. And they're, like, giggling away to each other, both obviously gagging for me, but basically still trying to decide among themselves which one of them is going to have me.

All of this was going on, roysh, while the rest of the goys were still up in the apartment, sleeping off their hangovers. You've got to get up early on holidays if you want to scope decent birds. These ones were up and out in the sun at, like, nine o'clock in the morning. You know the Spanish, they focking sleep for the best part of the working day. So two o'clock in the afternoon, roysh, bang in the middle of siesta time, the goys crawl out of the scratcher, come down to the pool and spend the next three hours moaning about how there's nothing here but ugly, milk-white birds from Knackeragua. There was no focking way I was telling them that there were two Spanish love goddesses staying in the Green Pork Apartments. Fionn must have copped my game though, because this particular morning, roysh, he arrives down to the pool about ten minutes after me. But I see him coming with his big focking sunburned head and his glasses, which he can't keep up on his nose with all the sweat, and I basically decide he's no threat to me. I'm like, 'I'm going to let you into a little secret, Fionn.' He goes, 'Does this have anything to do with your alarm clock ringing at half-eight the last three mornings?' I'm like, 'Sort of. There's these two birds, absolute stunners …'

And the next thing, roysh, out they come, flip-flopping their way in our direction, maybe heading for the sunbeds beside us, and I can see Fionn's focking glasses steaming up, so I'm like, 'Kool and the Gang, my man. Just play it Kool and the Gang.' And as they're passing, roysh, he goes, '*Olá, que tal?*' and I suddenly remember what he said to me on the flight on the way over. He was reading this book about Gran Canaria, roysh, and he looks up from it and he goes, 'I might actually use this holiday to polish up my Spanish,' and I was like, *What* a tosser! While I'm over here looking for my bit, roysh, he's looking for a focking Linguaphone course, and he is SO going to fock up my chances here it's not funny. But all of a sudden, roysh, the two birds stop and stort, like, blabbing away to him in Spanish. It's all, like, sangria and paella to me, but he's giving it loads back and the two birds are, like, really into it. He totally leaves me out in the cold, of course, so I'm like, 'Ahem, any chance of an introduction, Fionn?' And he goes, 'Sorry, this is Maria. And this is Rosa. This is my friend, Ross.' Maria says something to him in Spanish and the three of them break their shites laughing. Rosa, it turns out, is studying psychology as well, same as Fionn. A bird with a brain. I'm pretty relieved I didn't use my 'Will you rub some suntan lotion into my back?' line on them yesterday.

Then there's, like, five minutes more of blabbing away in Spanish, roysh, and then Fionn goes, 'I was telling Maria and Rosa that I'd love to explore the island. Maybe rent a car. The mountains are supposed to be breathtaking. There's finches there you won't find in any other part of the world. And Las Palmas is supposed to be a beautiful city, fantastic architecture.' I'm like, '*Hello?* I'm here to have a good time, for fock's sake,' and I look at Rosa, roysh, the one I've now decided I'm going to be with, and I throw my eyes up to heaven to sort of, like, take the piss out of him. But the two birds say something to him in Spanish, then the three of them, like, pick up their towels and Fionn goes, 'Well, the girls are on for exploring the island. We're going to go and see about renting that car,' and they all fock off, leaving me pretty much dizzy at how quick it happened.

Half an hour later, roysh, the rest of the goys arrive down, obviously on to my game as well. A couple of skangers pass by our spot and shout, 'THE POVERTY TRAP!' at us and JP high-fives the two of them. He's collecting focking disciples, that goy. They don't even know he's ripping the piss out of them. And then he storts on me. He goes, 'I was watching from the balcony, Ross. Looked to me like Fionn wiped your eye.' I'm like, 'Get a focking life.' He goes, 'Looks like you're coming back to the Jockey with us tonight.'

✳ ✳ ✳

Every night, roysh, before we go out on the lash, we have our dinner at the same place. It's, like, Salmonella City. The biggest buffet you've ever seen and it's, like, all you can eat for, like, seven euros. It has totally focked up my digestive system and I'm basically surprised the health authorities haven't closed the focking place down. Mind you, they won't need to, roysh, the way Oisinn is going through their food. It's the same craic every night. The owner, Fat Juan, takes our money on our way in and Oisinn points at him and goes, 'I am eating you out of focking business before I go home.' And Fat Juan laughs and goes, 'No way, Ireesh.' And Oisinn's there, 'It's a challenge, man. It's a challenge.'

✳ ✳ ✳

Actually, roysh, I have to take the blame for the state that Fionn's in. I did promise I'd get him back for stitching me up over the Spanish birds. When he got up this morning, he was full of it, going on about how he and Rosa and Maria were going to go and check out some, I don't know, focking banana plantation on the north of the island. He's taking the total piss out of me – doing it really, like, subtly, roysh – but taking the total piss all the same.

The birds came down for breakfast this morning and, alroysh, I admit it, roysh, I was trying to make myself sound more intelligent than I am, but what I said wasn't *that* stupid. I was just like, 'It's mad the way it's called the Canary Islands and you never, like, see any canaries.' Fionn translates this, roysh, and the three of them stort breaking their shites laughing for, like, twenty minutes. Fionn's like, 'Eh, Ross, the name of the islands is actually derived from *canis*, the Latin word for dog. The early explorers found many wild dogs here.' I'm going to shove that focking guide book up his orse.

Eventually, roysh, the birds go off to the supermarket to get, like, stuff for their trip, and I turn around to Fionn and I'm like, 'No hard feelings, man. Over–' He goes, 'Rosa and Maria? Are you sure?' I'm like, 'It's Kool and the Gang. Come on, I'll buy you a drink.' Now everyone knows, roysh, that Fionn can't handle the sauce. He's, like, locked on three pints. So we hit the bor and I stort, like, lorrying the drink into him and after, like, a few pints, roysh, he says he's going on to shorts, because he doesn't want to be too out of it for this trip. He's like, 'Vodka and orange,' and I'm basically ordering triple vodkas for the focker, with a little bit of orange just to, like, colour it. After three or four of those, he's totally forgotten about the banana plantation and me and him are, like, cruising the bors down by the beach. He's back on the pints and, being the sneaky bastard that I am, I'm drinking pints of non-alcoholic, which he doesn't cop.

So five o'clock, roysh, we end up back in the hotel bor with the others. It's weird, roysh, but pretty much everybody you meet on a knacker holiday claims to be friends with The Monk. Half his focking social circle must have been on our flight on the way over. This basically struck me while we were sitting there having a few scoops and we were joined by Eddie and Decker, these two blokes from Sheriff Street – or Shediff Stree – who were over with their wives. Anyway, roysh, Decker was basically saying how you had to hand it to Jackie Charlton, sure didn't he do an awful lot for the country but. And Fionn, roysh, who's basically off his tits by this stage, he goes, 'What are you bullshitting on about? Jackie focking Charlton!' And Eddie, roysh, it's like Fionn's just told him he's been, like, knobbing his bird or something, because he gives him this absolute filthy and he goes, 'Jackie Charlton put Ireland on de map!' And Fionn's there, 'Yeah, roysh. And cartographers all over the world woke up one morning and said, "Good God! Where the fock did that come from?"' and he storts laughing like a maniac. He's moved on to pina coladas, I notice. Eddie's like, 'Do ye tink usin' big wurds makes you better dan us?' and Decker pulls his mate across the table and tells him to leave it. He's there, 'Yer man's floothered, doesn't know wha' he's sayin'. And you don' wanna be banged up for anudder Christmas, do ye?' which suddenly has us all wondering. Christian catches my attention and, like, motions towards the door with his eyes, roysh, and Oisinn's looking pretty freaked-out as well. JP, of course, wants to stay, and there's, like, no way we can leave him to these two creamers. The goy seems to have a focking death wish on this holiday.

After the Jackie Charlton misunderstanding, roysh, Decker

tries to smooth things over by chatting in general about the holiday, 'For once in me bleedin' life, I'm glad we're after switching over to the euro, because the last time we was here, me and the wife spent the two weeks trying to get used to the Jaysusing money.' We all nod.

Eddie goes, 'Have yiz had de breakfast yet, lads?' I tell him I have. He goes, 'Not de same as at home, is it? De sausages are dem bleedin' hot dog tings. And de bacon? Jaysus, would ye go on ourra dat!' Decker goes, 'Tell dem what happened de furst day we came down but,' and Eddie goes, 'Ah Jaysus, yeah, I didn't know ye had to ask for de fry, so I'm there looking around de buffet – if dat's de right wurd – and it's all cheeses and fookin omelettes and potatoes. I says to de waiter fella – Manuel I call him, for de craic – I says to him, 'Potatoes? Dat's not breakfast, dat's a fookin dinner. Get inta dat fookin kitchen and fix us a fry-up dis minute.' Not de same but. Even de butter's too salty.'

Christian notices this book that Decker's been reading out in the sun. It's, like, *The General*. Or the Genoddle, as Decker calls him. 'Very good buke dat. Tell ye something but, he was a fookin dort burd, dat fella. Same as yer udder fella, Gilligan. A dorty-lookin' dort burd. Scumbags is all dee are. Now I'll tell ye sometin for nuttin, meself and Eddie there are very good friends with de Monk. He's a personal friend of mine. And a nicer fella ye couldn't meet. Very down to earth ...' Out of the corner of my eye, roysh, I can see Fionn getting ready to say something, and I'm not quick enough to stop him. He goes, 'He's a focking taxi driver!' Decker's like, 'Sorry, bud?' And Fionn goes, 'The goy drives a focking taxi for a living.' Eddie turns to me and he's like, 'Your mate's bang out of order, bud.' I'm like, 'Yeah, Fionn.

Kool and the Gang, my man. Kool and the Gang.' But Fionn goes, 'Down to earth? He's hardly focking Stephen's Green Club material, is he?' And then it's like, WHACK! Eddie decks him.

And even though I help Christian pick him up, roysh, and, like, Sellotape his glasses back together again, I'm basically happy that I've got him back. At least I think I have. The next thing I know, Maria and Rosa are in the bor and they're, like, all over him, hugging him and making sure he's alroysh and, like, screaming at me in Spanish. I get the gist of it. Bastard is pretty much the same in, like, any language. I'm there, 'I didn't hit him.' They're there, '*Bastardo! Bastardo!*' And he leaves with an arm around each of their shoulders.

Where are they taking him, I wonder. Their room?

✳ ✳ ✳

It's three o'clock in the afternoon, roysh, and I'm chatting up this absolutely cracking German bird – her name's, like, Mildred – and she's in the pool, roysh, swimming and whatever, and I'm sitting on the side with my feet in the water, basically listening to her bullshitting on about her plans to go Inter-railing for a year, while at the same time – and this is probably going to sound SO sleazy – trying to look down her bikini top. She's there, 'There is much in Europe I like to see. I am thinking I like to see Amsterdam and I like to see the Matterhorn and I like to see Prague …' and I'm going, 'Come over here and relax, Mildred. You'll get, em, cramp if you swim too long,' and she's like, 'I am so sorry, Ross. I am so excited when I start the talking about the Deutsche Bahn, yah?' She's actually a bit of a sap, roysh, and the goys have nicknamed her, 'Please To Help Me With My Rucksack?' but there's no denying she's a ringer for Angelina Jolie.

Anyway, roysh, there I am, sitting on the edge of the pool,

basically splashing her with water and it's, like, a major turn-on, and I'm just wondering whether she can see my stiffy in these shorts, roysh, when all of a sudden Oisinn comes up behind me and, like, pushes me into the pool, the fat bastard. Now I can't swim, roysh. I didn't tell Mildred this. I told her I was a pretty strong swimmer. And Oisinn, roysh, I presume he thought I was as well, at least I hope he did. So he dumps me in the water, roysh, we're talking the deep end here, and I sort of, like, flap my arms in the air for about a minute, totally freaking the shit, and then I sink straight to the bottom.

And in that moment, roysh, I thought that was it. My whole life, like, flashes in front of my eyes and shit. And weird stuff. I'm ten years old again, roysh, and I'm in the junior school and JP and Simon find out that I live in Sallynoggin – wasn't even Sallynoggin, it was Glenageary really – and they put it all over the school and JP and this gang of goys from sixth class stuff my head down the toilet next to the stationery stores and, like, flush it.

Then I'm twelve, roysh, and I'm in Irish college in Galway and it's half an hour after the *céili's* ended and I'm standing with my back to a gatepost and I'm getting my first snog off this bird called Martina from Boyle, County Roscommon, which I think might have been her full name because that's how she always introduced herself, and I'm there wearing the face off her, half my mind wondering what I'm supposed to do with my tongue, the other half wondering whether Oisinn and the rest of the goys will have horsed all the home-made bread by the time I get back to the house, then her *bean an tí* opens the front door and gives me daggers and I peg it back to the gaff before the ten o'clock curfew.

Then I'm fourteen, roysh, and I'm having my first drink, me

and Christian skulling a bottle of his old man's Sandeman port, then feeling dizzy, then puking our rings up in the downstairs jacks, both of us on our knees borfing into the same bowl, then falling asleep on the floor of the study and waking up in the spare room. Christian's old pair had carried us up to bed and they never said anything to my old man, in fact they never, like, mentioned it again.

Then I'm sixteen, roysh, and I'm meeting Sorcha for the first time at a porty in Fionn's gaff – he was basically going out with her cousin – and she was wearing a pink Ralph with the collar up, light blue jeans, which I think were Levi's, and Dubes, and she looked amazing, roysh, and we spent the whole night talking about everything – how I was hoping to make the Senior Cup team, how I hated my old pair, how I seriously needed grinds if I was going to do Honours economics for the Leaving – and we slept together in Fionn's sister's bed, roysh, and she told me she'd never done it before and I never told her that I hadn't either, and five minutes later, roysh, when it was all over, she storted crying and saying she was *such* a fool to do what she'd just done because I would never respect her now and I told her she was wrong, I was like, 'You are SO wrong.' Then I think of her crying on a few other occasions and me basically not giving a shit.

And then I'm nineteen and me and Christian's old dear are on the bathroom floor and … slap … SLAP … SLAPSLAPSLAP … Oisinn's slapping my face and he's shouting, 'WAKE UP! WAKE UP, YOU BASTARD!' and Fionn's pressing my chest and Christian's shouting, 'DON'T DIE. DON'T YOU FOCKING DIE.' And I can feel the cold, hard tiles against my back and I can hear Mildred sort of, like, borking orders, really calmly, and I can smell chlorine and I can taste vom in my mouth, and my stomach feels like it's about to burst, and I open my eyes just as Oisinn's about to give me mouth-to-mouth and I'm like, 'Don't even *think* about it, lover boy.' And all the goys break their holes laughing, roysh – relief, I suppose – and I roll onto my side and spend five minutes coughing and puking my ring up.

Oisinn goes, 'Fock it, Ross. Thought we'd lost you there.' And Mildred, roysh, she goes, 'But Ross, you told me that you are hoping to make it onto the Ireland swimming team for the Olympics.' And listening to her say it, roysh, I just break my shite laughing in her face and she goes, 'To tell lies is not so good, I am thinking,' and she storms off in a snot, and me and the goys basically collapse in laughter again.

✳ ✳ ✳

JP and Oisinn are having a row out on the balcony, roysh. Oisinn's there going, 'What you did was disgusting. There's no other word for it. You're so obsessed with knackers that you've become one yourself.' And JP goes, 'Cop on, Oisinn. Everyone pisses in the bidet.'

✳ ✳ ✳

By the second week of the holiday, roysh, we're all basically suffering from, like, malnutrition, so we all decide to head out for a meal in this, like, Indian, we're talking the Playa Tandoori or something, for the biggest feed you've ever seen. So there we are, roysh, lashing into the poppadoms and knocking back pints of Ken, trying to decide what we're going to have, and eventually, roysh, the goy comes to take our order and I go for the tandoori chicken tikka to stort and the chicken varutha curry for the main course. Fionn goes for the palak patta chat and the konkan seafood masala, obviously because they're the most difficult to pronounce, the focking show-off. Christian goes for the king prawns til tinka and the lamb korma, JP has no storter and the chicken tikka masala, and Oisinn orders the patrani machhi, the kadak seekh kebab, the masala dosa, two mixed tandoori platters, the beef chilli coconut fry, the chicken jalfreizi and the madras prawn thoku, all of which he will eat.

The food storts coming, roysh, and all of a sudden, out of the corner of my eye, I notice this, like, family arrive in, we're talking mum, dad, son and cracking daughter, we're talking Nelly Furtado's twin sister here, pretty, young, sixteen, seventeen, maybe eighteen, definitely borderline legal. And she cops me, roysh, I know she does, because I give her this, like, long look, roysh, and she looks straight back and when she sits down at the table, roysh, it's in a seat facing me.

Oisinn's lashing through his food, roysh, and he turns around to Fionn and he goes, 'This madras prawn thing I ordered,' and Fionn's like, 'What about it?' and Oisinn goes, 'Isn't *madra* the Irish word for dog?' Fionn's like, 'Don't eat it if it's bothering you. You've ordered pretty much everything else on the menu. I can't see you starving,' and Oisinn's just there, 'Remind me, who was it that won the UCD Iron Stomach competition three years in a row?'

And this bird, roysh, she's still giving me the mince pies and you have to feel sorry for her, being at that difficult age where her old pair can't accept that she's not a little girl anymore and she wants to hang out with, like, lads, not her knobhead parents. And they do look like knobs, all serious and everything. The poor girl basically can't take her eyes off me, roysh, so I give her a little smile and she gets a beamer and looks away.

JP is knocking back his sixth pint and saying we probably

should take it easy tonight what with the final of the water polo competition tomorrow. Our team, The D4s – Dumb, Ditsy and Dependent on Daddy – are supposed to be playing The Mun – or the Shower from the Towers, as Fionn calls them – at midday in the hotel pool, but right now the match is far from our thoughts. The food and the pints are going down well.

The bird, roysh, she's looking over again and she smiles back at me and then goes all shy again, roysh, and her old man has copped what's going on because he turns around in his seat and I just pretend to be really interested in some shite that JP's spouting now about Paddy and Tony, two friends he's made from Finglas. He says they've invited him to some club or other they go to on the first Tuesday of every month, basically family allowance day, when there are loads of loose single mothers out looking for a man. Mickey Tuesday, the lads call it. JP goes, 'I told them I'd certainly take the idea off-line. Push it out of an airplane, see if its parachute's good.'

The bird, roysh, I can feel her eyes on me again and when I look over at her this time, I blow her a kiss, roysh, but – FOCK – her old dear notices and the next thing she's looking at the daughter and then back at me and then at the daughter again and then she storts giving out shite to her. The old man, roysh, I watch him take his napkin off his lap and throw it down on the table really, like, angrily. Then he gets up, roysh, and comes over to our table. The goys, roysh, they hadn't copped what was going on – and I wasn't going to tell them in case they wanted in on the action – and they're all, like, totally mystified when the old man storts giving out yords to me. He's like, 'Would you mind not staring at my daughter like that. You're making her uncomfortable,' and I'm just there, 'Really?

She doesn't seem uncomfortable to me,' and he goes, 'Keep your eyes away from our table or I'm going to call the manager.'

And when he focks off, roysh, we all break our shites laughing and it's, like, high-fives all round.

✱ ✱ ✱

The D4s were soundly beaten in the final of the water polo competition. We were all too hungover to keep scores, but Andy – our asshole of a tour rep – said it was a record defeat.

✱ ✱ ✱

It's two o'clock in the afternoon and there's this, like, banging on our door and all this shouting in Spanish outside, and I presume it's the hotel security guard, wanting to know who focked a box of Frosties off our balcony into the swimming pool a few minutes ago. I don't even know why I did it. I've had a few scoops but I'm not, like, ossified or anything. Probably just boredom. I answer the door, roysh, and the goy's there, like, screaming his head off and, like, pointing at me. He's got a sort of, like, truncheon thing hanging from his belt, which he keeps pointing to as well. I'm just like, 'No focking comprende.' And then, roysh, I'm pretty proud of this because it came to me, like, out of the blue, I just go, 'They're grRREAT!' and slam the door in his face.

It probably isn't the end of the matter, but then again, roysh, I think the management have pretty much given up on us and are, like, counting the days until we basically leave. Looking around the gaff, you can't really blame the maids for refusing to clean the place. We've basically wrecked the apartment. There's, like, beer all over the floor, the toilet's blocked, thanks mainly to the chef at Salmonella City, and the bed sheets look like they've been through a focking dirty protest. It's like being back in Ocean City on a J1er. I'm like, 'This place looks like a bomb's hit it.' And Christian goes, 'If a bomb hit this place it'd cause thousands of pounds worth of improvements.' He can be a funny bastard, Christian.

I don't even know how the place got into this state. Me and Christian are basically the only ones who are ever here. Fionn's basically moved in with the two Spanish birds. He sleeps there every night and comes back in the morning to get, like, clothes for the day. There's only his suitcase left here now. When he comes in, roysh, he just, like, looks around the place as though it, like, disgusts him. I'll say this for the focker, though, he's looking well. Tanned, well-fed, the whole lot. The two birds are probably cooking for him as well as everything else. No all-you-can-eat-for-seven-euro shit-holes for him. I'd probably have a good tan myself, but I've had the serious Leon Trotskys for a week now, and the colour is running out of my face quicker than I can get it in. I've storted, like, calling Fionn 'Jack Duckworth' because of the sticky tape holding his glasses together, but then he just storts singing, 'Whenever, wherever, we're meant to be together ...' I made the mistake of telling him that Rosa looks like Shakira. On his way out, he always goes, '*Buenos noches,*' which probably means loser or something.

As for Oisinn and JP, they've pretty much moved out as well and are basically sleeping their way around the resort in this, like, competition they're having. Instead of the usual craic – seeing who can score more birds – the challenge is to get your bit in as many different hotels and apartment blocks as you can. They've got this, like, chart on the wall for keeping score. Beside every, like, entry, roysh, there's the name of a bird, when supplied, and a little comment:

THE SHAGATHON

Conqueror	Conquest	Location	Comment.
Ross	Sandra	Hotel Capri	She seemed pleased enough the following Morning
Ross	Jacinta	Playa del Sol	All night long, baby!
JP	Sharon from Finglas	The Green Field	
JP	Celine	The Doncel	Blonde bird who looks like Rebecca Romijn-Stamos
JP	???	Hotel Buena-ventura	Frizzy perm, works in Woodies
JP	Tanya	Tisalaya	Woody Woodpecker tattoo
JP	Linda from Donaghmede	Agaete Park	Standards slipping fast!!
JP	Tina	Las Arenas	Back on message with this Louise Redknapp lookalike
JP	???	Tanife	A rake with lipstick from Cobra who forgot she put burgers on + nearly burnt the place down!
JP	Cate with a C from Bayside	Roque Nublo	'What the fock is a girl like you doing on an island like this?'

Conqueror	Conquest	Location	Comment.
Oisinn	???	The Green Field	Red-haired friend of Sharon from Fingla's, what a boiler!
Oisinn	???	Koka	Bird from Clondalkin whose catchphrase is, 'Ah Jaysus, I'm sweatin'.'
Oisinn	Sally, I think	Hotel Buenaventura	Frizzy perm, Woodies, JP's sloppy seconds
Oisinn	Linda	Roque Nublo	Dream of Tallafornication!.!
Oisinn	Celia	Las Gacelas	19. Highly fertile. 3 kids and counting, 'Condoms are useless against this girl, captain.' Lagging jacket advised!
Oisinn	Shona	Los Gondolas	Caprice lookalike — a rare error of judgement, won't happen again
Oisinn	Sabrina	Green Park	Back to my best with a total moonpig
Oisinn	Claire — possibly ??	Vista Oasis	Bird from Navan with annoying laugh
Oisinn	Joan, according to her tattoo anyway	The Doncel	Fat bird who looks like Fizz off Coronation Street
Oisinn	???	Andalucia Park	Fat bird who looks like Fred Elliott off Coronation street

JP is obviously a bit pickier than Oisinn but, as Oisinn always says, it's quantity that counts, not quality. Five nights left and there's everything to play for still. Christian's, like, reading the chart over my shoulder. He's like, 'Holy shit, they move through this place any faster and they're going to have to start heading down the coast, maybe down to Maspolomas.' I'm like, 'They'll be home soon to fill in last night's results.'

Christian picks up on the jealousy in my voice. He goes, 'So what happened to you? You were in the game for a couple of nights and then you, like, dropped out.' I'm like, 'Well, it's not really me, is it?' He hands me a beer and goes, 'Don't give me that shit, Ross. It's TOTALLY you. You'd the Hotel Capri and the Playa del Sol apartments on the scoreboard before the rest of us had the tops off our suntan lotion. You were like a dog out of the traps.' I'm like, 'I know.' He goes, 'So, what happened?' I take a long slug out of the can. I'm like, 'Christian, this is something I don't want you to tell the goys, roysh?' He goes, 'I'm the best friend you've got, young Skywalker.' I'm like, 'You remember that bird I pulled in the Hawaiian Tosca that night?' He goes, 'The one with the dreadlocks?' I'm like, 'No, the second night. The one with the big hoopy earrings.' He goes, 'What about her?' I'm like, 'Well, we went back to her apartment, roysh, in Playa del Sol and ... well, this is going to sound weird, roysh, but it felt, I don't know, wrong or something.' He goes, 'Wrong?' I'm like, 'Yeah. For the first time in my entire life, I couldn't ... well, you know ...' He nods. He's like, 'I know alroysh. Been there. I was that Stormtrooper.' I'm like, 'Well, she basically threw me out of the apartment.' He's like, 'Just because you couldn't get a John Stalker?' I'm there, 'It wasn't that. I, em ... I let another girl's name slip.' He goes, 'Sorcha?' I nod. He's like, 'While you were ...' I'm like, 'No, no. It was in my sleep. I was saying her name in my sleep apparently. Don't know why, she wasn't even in my focking dream.'

He goes, 'You've still got it bad for the girl?' and I'm like, 'I didn't realise how bad, Christian.' He goes, 'What are you going to do?' I'm like, 'What can I do? She's in Australia. It's practically the other side of the world. And I don't even know if she's still with that tool of a boyfriend of hers.' He goes, 'You must be totally bummed out.' I'm like, 'TOTALLY. By the way, my congratulations.' He goes, 'For?' I'm like, 'Lauren. You haven't done the dirt on her.' He goes, 'I really like her, Ross.' I'm like, 'You must. We're in focking Playa del Ingles, Christian. It's, like, Shag City, Arizona. I mean, if you don't get your Nat King Cole here, customs give you a hug on the way home. And you've stayed faithful. You must love her.'

He goes, 'There's only one girl I ever loved.' I expect him to say Princess focking Leia or someone from *Star Wars*, Chewbacca the Wookie or something, but this is one of those rare nights when Christian is on planet Earth. He goes, 'Hazel.' I'm like, 'Hazel? From Mount Anville? Holy shit, Christian, you went out with her when you were, like, sixteen.' He goes, 'Fifteen.' I'm like, 'You were only with her for, like, three months?' He goes, 'Two.' I'm there, 'Didn't you break it off with her, though?' He goes, 'I caught her looking at another goy one day. No, it wasn't that she looked at another goy, it was the *way* she looked at him. See, she'd never looked at me like that before. And I knew she never would. And when you catch your bird looking at somebody the way she looked at him, well, there was no way it was ever going to be the same again.'

I don't know why, but I think this bloke he's talking about might have been me.

The goys suddenly arrive back, roysh, and JP's telling Oisinn all about the gaff he ended up in last night, going, 'It was a low-rise, bungalow-style setting, with ocean frontage and an extensive range of in-house amenities, surrounded by subtropical foliage. Rooms both modern and tasteful, with twenty-four-hour room service available ...'

Oisinn sees me and Christian sitting at the table having a beer. He's like, 'What are you two faggots talking about?'

* * *

Spanish beer is basically piss.

* * *

We're on the lash all afternoon, roysh, down by the pool and after, like, six or seven pints, my focking back teeth are floating, so I hit the jacks, the one in the bor, and there's basically two urinals, roysh. Decker's at one, jarred off his head judging by the way he's holding onto the wall with his free hand. Then there's the one beside it. There's also two traps with, like, proper toilets in them, but the floor in trap one is covered in piss and I'm wearing, like, flip-flops, and I happen to know the one in trap two is a knob-chopper and you have to hold the seat up with your hand while you take a slash. So I've no choice but to head for the urinal beside Decker. I don't think he recognises me. He goes, 'Alright, bud? Enjoyin' de holiday, are ye?' He definitely doesn't recognise me. He goes, 'Tell ye sometin, for de furst time in me bleedin' life, I'm glad dee brought dat euro in ...' I try to piss as quickly as I can, roysh, to get away from him, but it's no good. I've got a focking gallon of Ken in me. Decker seems to have stopped going, but he's, like, kept his position and decides to tell me his focking life story.

Anyway, I won't bore you with it. Except the last bit. He's only really in the Canaries, he says, because his claim has just come through. Eighteen grand, he tells me. He's there, 'Says I to the wife, "It's not gonna be like me redundancy money. We're gonna spend dis properly. We're goin on de holiday of a lifetime. Get yisser cases packed." Dat's how we ended up comin'. Eddie's me brudder-in-law, he's Sandra's brudder. Says I to herself, "I'm takin' de four of us off on de holiday of a lifetime." Sure it's better dan pissin' it up again de wall, isn't it?'

✳ ✳ ✳

You wouldn't be able to tell, roysh, but Oisinn's been going out with this bird for, like, a month. Hailey's her name. Not the Mae West lookswise, but a stunner by his standards. She was a real golden goal effort. He pulled her right at the end of the night, roysh, the time of the evening when you're basically cruising bus stops and focking Abrakebabras to score. Anyway, roysh, he books this holiday with us a couple of months back and, like, didn't have the balls to tell her he was going. So, like, three or four days before we're due to leave, roysh, he sort of, like, engineers this row with her over something that is, like, totally trivial. So he tells her he needs some space, some time to himself and suggests a two-week trial separation, roysh, just so he can, like, get his head together and shit. Now, roysh, at the very end of the holiday, his conscience is at him, judging by the way he's buying up, like, half the focking duty free shop in the shopping centre down by the beach. He's bought her, like, earrings and a ring, a new Discman, two T-shirts and a new camera, roysh, and then he hits the perfume section and he just stops all of a sudden and goes, 'Take in those beautiful aromas, goys. We're talking Lancôme, we're talking Elizabeth Arden, we're talking Thierry

Mugler, we're talking Jean-Paul Gaultier. If that's not enough to get the old olfactory senses going, I don't know what is.' What a weirdo. To him, this place is a brothel.

✳ ✳ ✳

The last night, roysh, we all end up in The Irish Jockey. I wanted to go to the Hawaiian Tosca again, but I lost the vote. JP's still on his take-the-piss-out-of-creamers buzz, Oisinn loves watching him in action and Christian basically doesn't give a shit where we end up. As for Fionn, roysh, his two Spanish honeys went home this morning and he votes for The Irish Jockey basically just to piss me off.

JP storts, like, straight away. The second he's in the door, roysh, he shouts, 'THE POVERTY TRAP!' and all the skangers stort, like, cheering and shouting it back. 'THE POVERTY TRAP! THE POVERTY TRAP!' There's a band playing, *My heart is in Ireland, that's where I long to be. Her hills and her valleys, are calling to me.'* This bloke, roysh, the kind of goy you wouldn't make eye contact with if you caught him staring at you on O'Connell Street at ten o'clock on a Friday night, he comes over, roysh, and he's like, 'Storee?' And JP's, like, really focking hamming it up with the accent again, going, 'Oh, I say. Hello there, Kellyer.' Oisinn is, like, breaking his shite laughing in his face, but the goy's too focking thick to cop it. JP, like, patronises him for a few minutes, then offloads him on me, telling him that I'm a huge Dublin football fan.

He turns to me and he's like, 'Whaddya tink of da way Tommy Carr was treated?' I'm pretty sure that Tommy Carr used to be, like, the manager of Dublin. I wonder to myself, is Kellyer a fan or not? My life could depend on the answer I give him. I decide to, like, bluff it. I'm there, 'That's, like, the sixty-four-thousand-dollar question. It's the one we all want answered.' He seems to be happy with this because he drops the subject. He goes, 'Furst ting I do when I get off da plane is I'm goin' straight inta town and gettin' chips wi' curry sauce. Have ye had da curry sauce over here? Fookin brutal, man. Brutal. Sure steak and chips is all I've eaten since I got here, ask any of da lads.' Then, roysh, completely out of the blue, for no reason at all, he tells me that his brother is in the IRA, and that if I ever want anyone shot to give him a shout and it's sorted. *'Though born here in this land, my heart is in Ireland. The land of the old folk, is calling to me.'* I manage to attract Fionn's attention, roysh, and I tell him what Kellyer said to me and he just laughs. He goes, 'Focking hell, you're white as a ghost. Ross, the IRA is a covert terrorist army, organised around a system of cells to maintain secrecy. If he told you his brother's in the IRA then the chances are he's not. Come on, it's your round.'

Everyone's shouting, 'THE POVERTY TRAP!' JP's up at the bor. He's still wearing the football shirt that he's had on since the first night we arrived, but he's drinking large brandies and smoking cigars and shouting, 'AFFLUENCE! AFFLUENCE!' really ripping the piss now. Then everyone storts shouting, 'AFFLUENCE!' JP storts telling this other skanger – Anto from Ballyfermot – that he's going to get a tattoo before he goes home tomorrow, roysh, and Anto suggests a skull painted in the colours of the Irish flag – 'green, whoy and yelli' – with barbed wire on it. And JP goes, 'And explosions in the background. I simply must have explosions in the background.' *'And it's off to Dubbalin in the green (fuck the Queen), where the bayonets glisten in the sun (fuck the hun) ...'* Fionn is chatting up this Spanish barmaid. He's like, *'Olá, que tal?'* I hear Christian telling Oisinn that it's just like the Mos Eiseley cantina and then they both shout, 'THE POVERTY TRAP!' and I am SO focking scared.

✳ ✳ ✳

Probably the best craic of the entire holiday, roysh, is seeing Oisinn and JP at the airport on the way home, trying to get away from all the birds they've been knobbing for the last, like, fortnight, without giving them their addresses and phone numbers. This bird, roysh, she asks JP for his number and he goes, '90210,' and the bird's like, 'That's very short.' He's like, 'You may need to put a two in front of that now.' She goes, 'It's still a number short,' and he's like, 'Then add an eight as well.' She goes, 'At the beginning or the end?' and he's like, 'I'm easy.'

Oisinn tells this fat bird – it has to be the Fred Elliot lookalike – that his address is, like, 1 Main Street, Foxrock, Dublin 18. She's like, 'You're a liar,' really, like, aggressive and he goes, 'I'm not, that's where I live.' She goes, 'I bet your real name isn't really Kevin either.' Oisinn's like, 'It is, I swear.' And she turns around to JP and she goes, 'Martin, tell me the truth, is that his real address?'

CHAPTER FIVE
The One Where Ross Lets The Cat Out Of The Bag

I get back from holidays, roysh, and I check my messages. A girl called Debbie has rung, roysh, to ask me – 'OH! MY! GOD! you are going to think I am *such* a freak of nature' – whether I might have accidentally taken her *Chill Out Moods* CD, 'because it was on the locker beside the bed when you … no, forget it. Oh my God, I am, like, SO embarrassed.' It's a shit album anyway, can't imagine her missing it. Oh and Michelle from Ulster Bank has called to say she's sorry that I didn't, like, make it to some meeting I don't even remember agreeing to, to discuss the SSIA, 50-50 funds, projected investment growth and loads of other bollocks I basically don't understand.

✱ ✱ ✱

For the last few weeks, roysh, I've basically had this, like, verruca on the sole of my foot, and I'm pretty sure I know where it came from as well. These are the things that your travel agent should warn you about before you go off on a knacker holiday, but they don't. I reckon basically I got it from that goy from Sheriff Street, the one with, like, the tricolour hanging over the edge of his balcony. I tell this to Fionn, who I make the mistake of, like, confiding in one night, roysh, while we're in the gaff watching 'The Villa'. He's like, 'A tricolour? Ross, that could be any one of fifty people.' I'm like, 'You remember him. *"Did you see our Joanne winning the karaoke last night, what? Sex bomb, sex bomb …"'*

He goes, 'Got you now. Why him, though?' I'm like, 'I just know. Fock, what am I going to do?' He's like, 'Hey, why are you telling me this shit anyway?' I'm there, '*Hello?* You're the one in college, remember?' He goes, 'Ross, I'm doing psychology.' I'm like, 'And?' He goes, '*And* you need a doctor. Why not go to see old what's-his-name?' I'm like, '*Hello? Earth to Fionn.* I've spent the last six months trying to get into his daughter's knickers. I hardly think she's going to be interested when she finds out I've got this big festering sore on my foot.' And he goes, 'Ross, she'll just have to accept you … warts and all.' Then he storts, like, breaking his shite laughing. Dickhead.

I'm like, 'Fionn, you better not breathe a *word* about this to anyone.' He's like, 'What do you take me for, Ross?' And I go out into the kitchen, roysh, and pull out the phone book and stort looking up doctors. I can't go to the local GP for reasons already explained, and knowing my luck, I'd probably run into the old dear in the waiting room, picking up her focking HRT, and I can very nearly hear her already. 'Oh the shame of it, Ross! There hasn't been a verruca in our family for *seventeen* generations.' You know the way she goes on.

And anyway, roysh, it's got to be a doctor with experience of treating verrucas. The way I see it, roysh, no GP from up our way is likely to have ever seen one. It has to be a doctor from a Ken Acker area. I eventually find one in Newtownmountkennedy, roysh, and after taking the CD player out of the cor, I hit the dual carriage-way, and the next thing I know, I'm sitting in a waiting room with some total focking AJH grilling me about my business, basically a receptionist who thinks she's a focking doctor. She's like, 'And what shall I say your problem is?' I just, like, whisper, 'A verruca,' and she's like, 'A VERRUCA?' at the top of her voice. I'm, like, looking around me. There's these two women behind me, skangers basically, and they stop talking when they hear the word. I'm like, 'Why don't you put an ad in the focking *Herald*?' I sit down, roysh, and I stort getting really paranoid. I've knobbed quite a few birds from out this direction and I keep thinking some-one's going to, like, come in and recognise me.

I'm listening to these two birds and it's all, 'Oh yeah, I'm a martyr to me back, Mary. Always have been.' And when the doctor goes, 'NEXT,' I just get up and go in ahead of them, even though I'm not next. The two women stort muttering to each other, roysh, and one of them plucks up the courage and goes, 'Excuse me,' trying to put on a posh voice, 'Excuse me, you're after skipping the queue.' She's basically trying to embarrass me. I'm like, 'Yeah? Tell it to focking Adrian Kennedy, you knacker.'

I go into the doctor, roysh, and it's, like, pleasantries and shit and then it's like, 'What seems to be the problem?' I'm like, 'It's a bit, em ... embarrassing.' He goes, 'Is it a sexually transmitted disease? HERPES? SCABIES? URETHRITIS? SYPHILIS?' I'm like, 'What is it with people in here? Would you mind not shout-ing?' He's there, 'GONORRHOEA? CHLAMYDIA? I KNOW MY STDs.'

I'm like, 'It sounds like you do. Look, I've got a verruca.' He goes, 'A verruca?' looking all, like, disappointed and shit. He's like, 'A verr-u-ca.' I'm like, 'Yeah, what happened was I picked it up on a knacker holiday.' He goes, 'Yes, that and a lot more besides, I'd wager. Well, verrucas are actually quite common ...' I'm there, 'Not where I come from, they're not.' He goes, 'Infection of the skin caused by the human papilloma virus ... can be quite painful ... often picked up in swimming pools and the like ... would disappear itself if you left it, but if it's troubling you, it's best to act.

'Here,' he goes, handing me this prescription, 'slop this stuff on it a couple of times a day. It'll clear up in a week ... now, any sexually transmitted diseases to report?' I'm like, 'No.' He goes, 'CHANCROID? TRICHOMONIASIS?' I get up and get the fock out of there and I can hear the goy still shouting this stuff after I've left the surgery.

The stuff smells focking vile. It's, like, some kind of acid, roysh, but I lash on the old *Gio Acqua Di* before I go out that night so nobody will smell it. I hit Kiely's and there I am, roysh, having a few scoops, and I notice that the goys are being really, like, weird around me. It's all, 'How are you feeling, Ross?' and, 'Everything okay?' Even the birds are like, 'Oh my God, I didn't think you'd be drinking.' And I'm storting to wonder, roysh, whether Fionn's actually said something.

So anyway, roysh, about half an hour into the night, I've got to go and, like, drain the snake, so I get up from the table and head for the jacks. That's when I hear this, like, ringing, roysh, and basically everyone in the entire pub stops whatever it is they're doing and storts, like, staring at me. So I look down, roysh, and it turns out that some focker – probably Oisinn, the fat bastard – has tied a bell onto my ankle when I wasn't looking. And all the goys are standing up, giving it, 'UNCLEAN! UNCLEAN!'

Basically assholes.

✳ ✳ ✳

I hate cats. We're talking TOTALLY here, and I wouldn't use that word lightly. The problem with cats is that you could spend an hour petting one, roysh, and then the thing'll get bored with you, scratch your arm, fock off out the window and not come back for two weeks. Once someone else is feeding it, that is. I focking *hate* them. But Oreanna, roysh, this bird I was kind of seeing sort of, like, on and off for a few weeks, she *loves* them. Most birds basically do.

Anyway, this one she had, roysh, was called Simba, an evil, orange little thing. The focker could open doors, I'm telling you, and materialise through, like, walls and shit. There we'd be, roysh, me and Oreanna, getting jiggy on her sofa and, like, the cat would be outside on the window ledge, roysh, pawing away at the glass, basically trying to get in. Next thing you'd look down, roysh, and the thing was there at your feet, staring up at you and, like, hissing.

Simba hated me, roysh, and basically that's the thing about cats. They get, like, really, really jealous if they think you're, like, moving in on their patch. They're big into, like, territory and shit, or so Fionn says, and he spends a lot of time in the gaff watching the Discovery Channel. Me and Oreanna would be sitting there in front of the telly, roysh, getting it on, hands busy with her bra strap, and the focking thing would jump up on the sofa and, like, squeeze in between the two of us, and of course Oreanna, roysh, the total sap, she'd go, 'OH! MY! GOD! isn't he SO cute. And SO clever.' She could only ever see good in the little bastard.

There was this one night, roysh, when we were in her gaff in Greystones, watching 'Big Brother', which is, like, her favourite programme, roysh, and all of a sudden Simba storts, like, licking my hand, and at first, roysh, I thought he was actually trying to make friends with me. Turns out he was, like, tenderising my flesh before he sank his teeth into me.

So I storted making up all these stories, roysh, which I told Oreanna I'd read in the paper, about old dears who'd, like, died in their gaffs and their bodies had been found a week later and they'd been, like, half eaten by their cats. And Simba would sit there staring at me while I said this, roysh, and, I focking swear to God, that animal understood every word I was saying. I was, like, wasting my breath, though, because basically it did nothing to change Oreanna's mind. So instead, roysh, now and then I'd try to persuade her to make me a cup of tea and, when she was out in the kitchen, I'd try to hit the thing with the odd sly kick. The bastard was usually too fast for me though. I said usually.

Because basically where all of this is going, roysh, is that this one particular night, the night me and Oreanna finished with each other funnily enough, I was swinging the old Golf GTI into her driveway and I felt this, like, bump under the cor. And I knew straight away, roysh, what I'd done. For once in his life, the focker just wasn't quick enough for me. I swear to God, it was an accident, though Oreanna was never going to believe that, especially after all the threats I'd made against the thing. I got out of the cor and, like, checked the damage. At first I thought there was, like, an actual scratch on the fender, roysh, but it turned out it was only a bit of fur, stuck on with blood.

I'm not being a dickhead, roysh, but the cat didn't suffer. Had he still been alive, I'd have had to finish him off with the cor jack, which *so* wouldn't have been a pretty sight. Of course, none of that would have been any consolation to Oreanna, so I decided not to tell her, one because she'd be too upset, roysh, and two because it would lessen my chances of getting my bit that night. So what I did, roysh, was I slapped the thing into the boot of the cor and decided to drive home later through Bray and fock the thing in the Dargle. She'd be pretty heartbroken when old Simba didn't come home, roysh, but she'd just presume it'd gone off to live with some old biddy who fed him, I don't know, cake or chocolate. I'd be sure to suggest it.

So I went into the gaff, roysh, acted natural, the whole lot. Her old pair were in Villamoura, playing golf. And she puts on this video, roysh, and it's, like, *Cats*, the focking musical. I have to say, roysh, I felt like *such* an asshole at that moment, but there was nothing I could do. Anyway, roysh, we ended up having a really great chat, I was telling her all about this gaff I just sold down the road from her in Delgany for, like, four hundred grand, and she was telling me about how she may have to go back to wearing a brace for six months, depends what the orthodontist says on Monday. I don't think I need to go into detail about what happened next, roysh. Not being, like, big-headed or anything, but I basically ended up staying the night. I'll spare you the details, roysh, but basically we're talking, TOUCHDOWN!

The next morning, roysh, she brings me a fry in bed, the whole lot, we're talking sausages, bacon, egg, mushrooms, toast, and I'm there going, Have I struck gold here or what? As she gets out of the shower, roysh, she asks me whether I could drop her off at work. She works in some, like, building society in Bray. I have to say I was a bit pissed off about having to get up so early, roysh, but I play it cool like Huggy Bear and half an hour later, roysh, I'm sitting in the cor, with the engine ticking over, waiting for her to lock up the house, put the alarm on, blah blah blah.

She opens the passenger door, roysh, and she goes, 'Ross, what's that smell?' I'm there, 'I don't know. I think it's the exhaust. I'll have to get it looked at.' So she had this bag with her, roysh, because she was playing tennis after work with Megan, who's, like, her best friend, and she goes, 'I'll just put this in the boot.' And that was when I remembered what the smell was. But it was too late to do anything at that stage.

Oh *my* God, you should have heard her screams. Half of focking Greystones did. People storted, like, coming out of their houses. She's there going, 'He killed Simba. He killed Simba.' I have to say, roysh, that the cat was not a pretty sight at that stage. We're basically talking, like, *rigor mortis* here. Its teeth were showing, its eyes were, like, rolled backwards into its head and there was, like, a few bluebottles buzzing around where the blood … you get the picture.

I actually thought the neighbours were going to, like, lynch me, they were all there looking at me like I was, I don't know, focking Fred West or someone. I'm just there, 'Spare me, will you? It was a focking accident.' And this old dear, roysh, a real shit-stirrer, she takes off her coat and puts it over Oreanna's shoulders and she says to come with her, she'll make her a cup of tea. And as she's sort of, like, walking her off, roysh, I go, 'Oreanna, text me later, after tennis.' And this old dear, a real bitch, roysh, she turns around and goes, 'I don't think you should show your face around here ever again.'

And I watch them disappear into this old dear's gaff, roysh, and that's when I realise that they're all still there, all the neighbours, staring at me in, like, total disgust, and I mean TOTAL. And this one goy, roysh, a real Ned Flanders dickhead, he goes,

'Pamela's right. We don't want to see you around here again.'
And I go totally apeshit at that, roysh. I grab the cat – or what's
left of it – out of the boot and basically slap it down on the
ground in front of him and all this, like, blood and shit splashes
all over his shoes and his Farah slacks and I'm there – and I'm
actually pretty proud of this, roysh – I'm there, 'You focking bury
it then, Flanders, if you're so smart.'

∗ ∗ ∗

*Modern décor. FTB. Owner occupier. Section focking 23. Double-fronted.
Architecturally acclaimed. Villa-style. Ease of access. Work-from-home
spacious.* I come home from the office with my head wrecked
from all this shit. Been flogging these gaffs all week, roysh, out in
Gorey of all places – 'superb quality investments in village
setting, only 4,275 remain' – and they're going like hot cakes, but
it's, like, work, work, work at the moment and the last thing I
need when I get home is someone else wrecking my head.

Switch on my mobile and I've got, like, three voice messages.
Michelle from Ulster Bank – surprise, sur-focking-prise – really
does feel it's a shame that I've got all that money just sitting in a
deposit account when it could be working for me. She blabs on
for a bit about single premium investment schemes offering
unlimited growth potential, managed funds with one hundred
per cent capital protection, international shares and fixed-interest
securities and loads of other shite that gives me a headache. The
second is from this bird, Treasa, who's, like, second year actuarial
studies in UCD, who I ended up being with at Ultan's twenty-
first, and who basically, roysh, can't get over the fact that it was a
one-night stand, although she doesn't seem to have noticed that
her Celine Dion *Greatest Hits* album went walkies the night I was
in her gaff. So I was actually in a bit of a fouler after that, roysh,

until I heard the third message and that, like, really cheered me up. It was the old man, roysh, and at first I thought it was, like, more of his bullshit, please come home, we miss you, your mother's HRT isn't going well, blah blah blah. But it's not, roysh, it's like, 'Ross, disaster. Disaster with a capital D. The new neighbours. They're, well, they're not like us.'

He goes, 'Your mother and I went in to see them last night. Thought we'd give them a day or two to get properly settled in and whatnot. Didn't suspect a thing, of course. Not even when we saw them bringing in the big china collie dog and the bunk beds. *They're working class, Ross!* Oh, how could we have been so blind? We just jumped in there with two feet, of course. Called in with a card and one of your mother's almond and apricot roulades, welcome to the neighbourhood thank you very much indeed.

'Well, what a sight it was that greeted us. The man, oh I can hardly bring myself to say his name, Christy, he was in the front garden, working on the motor. His words, Ross, not mine. Working on the motor, if you don't mind. Oh, I put my foot in it, of course. Told him about Jim, the man who fixes my car. "Why would ye shell out a couple a hundred 'n' odd notes if you know how to fix it yisserself?" Sorry, your mother does the voice much better than I do. She's able to see the funny side of it. Sometimes. Although most of the time she just cries.

'Of course the woman, Cindy is her name, she comes out then. It's "Ah, Jaysus, Howiya," from her. Howiya indeed. I thought your mother was going to collapse on the spot. On the spot. With a capital, I don't know, S I suppose. And what did she say then? "Oh, you're after makin' us a lovely cake." Or cayik. Can't pronounce it the way she did. Your mother said, "It's not a cake. It's roulade." And this frightful Cindy person said, "It's a fookin cake where we come from, love."

'Which is God knows where. Lottery winners, no doubt. Not a job between them, I'd bet. In the pub from noon till night. Kids up to God knows what. Oh, the lottery. A curse, Ross, a bloody curse. I phoned Hennessy, but of course they've got the law on their side. Haven't actually done anything illegal, he said. "But they don't *belong* here," I told him. "It's wrong, damn it." Had to apologise to Hennessy for that. Out of order. God knows this hasn't been easy for any of us.

'But em … Ross … Eduard, you know, Eduard from the golf club, he says that Hook, Lyon and Sinker were the agents for that house. Em … you didn't have anything to do with selling it, did you? Of course you didn't. I mean I told your mother that. "This is Ross we're talking about," I said. He wouldn't … em … anyway, I'd better go. Who knows when it's all going to go off next door. Your mother's bought a pair of binoculars. Keep an eye on things. Damage is already done, I told her. Knocked about eighty thousand euros off the value of this place. And what's next? Heroin? Call-girls coming and going at all hours of the night? Drive-through shootings?'

Drive-through shootings. Is he a wanker or what?

✳ ✳ ✳

Alicia is this bird I know, roysh, we're talking the image of Lisa Faulkner here, but at the same time, roysh, as the goys always say, she's a bit like a shirt you'd buy from one of those skanger shops in the Ilac Centre: you only really get one good wear out of her. Anyway, roysh, that's neither here nor there. The point is that Oisinn has basically been on a promise with her for, like, six weeks – *Pleasures* by Estée Lauder, he calls her – and he was waiting for his old pair to go away to Bologna, so he could, like, have a porty in his gaff. Then his old dear goes and chokes on an organic strawberry, or gets food poisoning or some shit, and the trip is off and suddenly Oisinn is, like, putting pressure on me to throw a porty instead, we're talking in one of JP's old man's gaffs, one of the houses I'm supposed to be trying to sell. This all comes up in Conway's on the Thursday night. He goes, 'Come on, half of those houses are vacant. We'll go in, we'll porty and we'll be gone the next day after tidying up. JP's old man will never know.'

JP hasn't, like, heard any of this, roysh, because him and Fionn are in the middle of texting this joke to Ryle, and it's like, **WHAT'S THE DIFFERENCE BETWEEN RTE AND THE TITANIC? RTE HAS TWO ORCHESTRAS.** I didn't get it either, but when I stopped laughing, roysh, I asked JP what he thought about the idea of a porty, maybe in the gaff on Killiney Hill Road that's been on the books for focking ages, and he goes, 'Sounds like a plan, Ross. Sounds like a plan. Furnish me with updates,' which is basically Estate Agent for Yes.

So the night of the porty, roysh, we're talking the following Saturday night here, we're all in the gaff, all the goys, getting totally trolleyed. And when I say totally, roysh, I am *not* exaggerating. And all the birds, roysh, they're all in the next room, sitting around, trying to act all mature, going, 'Oh my God, *how* old are they supposed to be again?' They're pretty much feeling left out of things, roysh, because it's all the old goys off the S, knocking back the Ken, singing the old songs: 'The Mayor of Bayswater', 'On Top of Old Sophie', and 'Give me a Clone'.

Oh give me a clone, Of my own flesh and bone,
With the Y chromosome changed to an X.
Then when it is grown, My own little clone,
Will be of the opposite sex.

I head out to the kitchen to grab a beer and who's out there only Claire, as in the Dalkey wannabe from Bray, and Erika. Well, you know Erika, she's a total bitch at the best of times and she's giving Claire a hard time as per usual, telling her that there should be mandatory sentences for people who go around begging in pubs, knowing full well that Claire's doing, like, promotional stuff in pubs for Heineken at the moment. Claire goes, 'Obviously what I'm doing is—' and Erika just cuts her off, roysh, and goes, 'Claire, what you're doing makes you no better than a Romanian.'

And off Claire runs, roysh, bawling her eyes out, and Erika shouts after her, 'Your roots are showing, Dear.' I actually feel a bit sorry for her because Erika really knows how to get under her skin, but I'm just there, 'I like the way you handled that. About time someone told her.' Erika ignores this and looks around the kitchen. She goes, 'When I heard you were having a porty, Ross, I thought it was going to be in that little bedsit of an apartment that you and Fionn are sharing. I'm impressed. You're beginning to grow on me.' I'm like, Oh my God, I am SO in here. Anyway, roysh, I'm just about to make my move when all of a sudden the front door swings open and it's, like, JP and his old man. Hadn't actually noticed that JP was missing, roysh, and I know straight away what his game is. He's done a Judas on me, stitched me up big-style. For ages, roysh, he's been jealous of the fact that I'm basically better at the job than him and he's been trying to, like, shaft me, which he's obviously just done, and done it TOTALLY.

His old man walks up to me and he goes, 'Ross, did I or did I not tell you that I was trusting you with a set of keys and there was to be no parties?' I'm like, 'Basically, yeah.' He goes, 'Lies. Deceit. Going behind people's backs …' Then he just, like, smiles at me, roysh, and he goes, '… every test I set you, you pass it with flying colours. You have absolutely no sense of right and wrong. I struck oil when I found you, boy. Struck oil.' You should have seen JP's face. He just storms out, roysh, and I hand his old man a can of Ken and he cracks it open and turns around to Erika, looks her up and down – the goy is a total sleazebag – and he goes, 'Nice dress. Can I talk you out of it?'

✳ ✳ ✳

I come home from work, roysh, long hard day at the office, and I'm trying to watch 'Temptation Island', but Fionn's telling me about this coffee shop, roysh, it used to be called Kennedy's and now it's called Bon Espresso and Patisserie and I'm like, 'And your point is?'

✳ ✳ ✳

The knackers are going to have to go, lottery winners or not. The pigeon loft went up on Tuesday night, roysh, and that's what the old pair said when they saw it. They have *got* to go. Not that I give a fock one way or another what they say. I hadn't actually spoken to either of them since they focked me out of the gaff, but let's just say that suddenly what's in their interests is also in mine.

I was actually trying to watch 'Jackass' when the old man rang and I made the mistake of answering it before I checked who it was, so I ended up having to listen to him bullshitting on about this loft for, like, twenty minutes. He's there going, 'They're vermin, dirty bloody things that spread disease.' I'm like, 'It's only a few focking birds. Get over it.' He goes, 'I wasn't referring to the pigeons, Ross.'

And I can hear the old dear in the background, roysh, going, 'Tell him, Charles. Tell him. They will not be satisfied until they have turned this road into one of those *fearful* council estates. Why did they ever leave Coolock or wherever it is they came from?' I can hear the old man pouring himself a brandy, a double by the sounds of it. He goes, 'Your mother's right, Ross. The pigeon loft, the Nissan Bluebird, they're the thin end of the wedge. What's next? Horses wandering around the streets here?'

In the background, the old dear's going, 'Tell him about the Rottweiler, Charles. And the ice cream van.' The old man goes, 'Come on, we've no proof that it was an ice cream van.' And the old dear storts going apeshit, she's there, 'Charles, I've been to the northside. I *know* what an ice cream van sounds like.' He goes, 'All I'm saying, Darling, is that you were upset.' And she loses it then, roysh, she's like, 'I HEARD AN ICE CREAM VAN, CHARLES. WHY WON'T YOU BELIEVE ME?' I can hear him, like, hugging her, roysh, trying to calm her down, and listening to this bullshit, roysh, I end up missing this entire scene where Johnny Knoxville gets set on fire, which pisses me off, so I end up hanging up on him and switching the phone off for a couple of hours.

I found out later, roysh, that the second I hung up, their phone rang. And of course they thought it was me ringing back. The old dear answers it and the old man's there going, 'Ask him did we lose the signal this end or was it that end. This chap next door's probably got one of those blasted CB radios. You mark my

words.' But it wasn't me, of course. It was the skangballs themselves. And going by the old man's account, roysh, the old dear
was, like, basically in shock.

This *wan*, roysh, Cindy I think he said her name was, she's
asking her something, and you can just picture the old dear there
going, 'Yes … yes … tomorrow night? Em … I don't know …'
And the old man, who's copped who it is, roysh, he's there telling
her to, like, play it cool, go along with whatever she's saying. And
the old dear's there going, 'Em … I'll see … I'm not sure if I can
make it, but … okay … bye …' She hangs up, roysh, and the old
man's going, 'What was all that about?' And she's like, 'She
wouldn't take no for an answer, Charles. She's invited me to a
party. Tomorrow night. In her house.' The old man's there,
'You? On your own?' And the stupid bitch goes, 'Yes, she said
she's having *"a few of the girls"* around. Bit of a party. I tried to
make some excuse, but …' And the old man goes – now this is
according to him – he goes, 'Darling, you have to go. You really
do. Otherwise they'll think something's up. Just go and do your
best to act naturally and then, when I speak to Hennessy and we
hit them with the solicitor's letter – BANG! – they won't know
what day of the week it is. In the meantime, we've just got to act
as though everything's normal.'

And you can imagine the old dear, roysh, the stupid wagon
coming over all faint at the thought of it, and I have to say,
roysh, a video tape of her stepping through the front door of
that house would be funnier than anything that's ever been on
'Jackass'. She goes, 'I don't know if I can do this, Charles. I'm
not strong like you.' The old man's like, 'I know it'll take an
enormous effort, but …' She goes, 'Oh, I can just picture it,
Charles. The horror. Net curtains. Brass flower pots in the

windows. Clothes drying on radiators …' And the old man's there going, 'Darling, be brave. This could be our only chance to get rid of them. Once and for all.'

So basically, roysh, what happened was that at eight o'clock the next night, the dopey bitch pops in next door with a bottle of Chateâuneuf du Pape. According to the old man, when he saw the bottle of wine he went, 'Oh, good cover. I like it. You're thinking, Darling.' Before she left he checked she had her panic alarm with her, and then she was off. Two hours later, roysh, she was back, basically in focking tears. She just, like, fell into the old man's arms and he was like, 'It's over, Darling, it's over. You're home now. You're safe.' And she goes, 'You don't understand, Charles. It was a … oh, I can't even say the word.' He's like, 'Well, don't. Just try to forget about it.' She goes, 'No, I can't, Charles. I have to say it. It was a … a … a lingerie party.'

I can't keep the laughter in when the old man tells me this. She went, 'It was *awful*, Charles. Her friends, they're … animals. That's all you could call them. It was *Howiya* this and *Ah Jaysus* that. Frizzy hair and tight jeans …' And he turns around to her, roysh, and he goes, 'Try not to think about it.' She goes, 'And then the lingerie came out. Oh, it was horrid, Charles, *horrid*. And they knew. They knew how uncomfortable I was with it. Kept telling me to buy various things. Spice up your love life, they said. And they'd all laugh. Horrible laughter. I said I didn't have my credit card with me …' The old man tells her she might feel better after a shower and she goes, 'No, I have to tell you this, Charles. This Cindy woman, she said it didn't matter. She'd buy me this as a present,' and the old dear pulls this thing out of her pocket, roysh, and throws it on the table, and from the old man's description it basically sounds like a pair of red crotchless knickers with feathers on them. I am breaking my shite laughing when I hear this. I basically can't hold it in.

The old man, roysh, he's still bulling when he tells me all this on the phone. He goes, 'Ross, I have a job for you.' I'm like, 'I already have a job.' He goes, 'Well, call it a bit of moonlighting then. It's a special project and it's worth five grand to you. That's what I'll pay you to get those *animals* next door out. Within two months. And I don't care how you do it either.' I'm like, 'I'll do it. But don't think this means we're back playing happy families again. You can get that idea out of your head. But for five thousand bills, I'll take the job.' He goes, 'Two months, Ross.' And I'm there, 'Piece of piss.'

✱ ✱ ✱

Fionn says he only has one rule when it comes to the opposite sex, roysh, and that's never go out with a bird who lives on a Close. I'm like, 'Fionn, you have some seriously focked-up ideas.' He goes, 'Ross, have you ever known me to have trouble with the opposite sex?' and he actually has a point.

✱ ✱ ✱

I'm in Mullingar, roysh, and I'm not even sure what county it's in. All I know is that it took me two focking hours to get here and that JP's old man told me to refer to it as 'the gateway town of Mullingar', presumably to give the impression to the suckers I'm showing it to this afternoon that it's on the outskirts of Dublin. Of course, wouldn't you know it, Mr and Mrs Nugent are already there at the gaff when I get there, roysh, both of them already bulling. The goy goes, 'Well, we've already spotted the first untruth in the prospectus.' I'm like, 'Sorry I'm late,' trying to subtly change the subject, but he's there, 'Forty-five minutes from Dublin, it says here. In what, a Lear jet?' I'm there trying to remember some of the killer lines I learned earlier. I go, 'The strategic radial corridor should slash commuting times ...' but the focker's too quick for me, roysh, he's obviously been swotting up, and he's there, 'By *strategic radial corridor* I presume you're referring to the N4?' I'm there, 'Em ... yeah.' He goes, 'We *took* the N4. And I can only presume the N stands for nights, as in it'll take you the best part of four bloody nights to get home.'

I'm there, 'Hey, I'm getting majorly negative vibes here. If you don't want the house ...' His wife, roysh – not bad looking, a little bit like Emma Forbes, D&G coat, Burberry scarf, cracking on she's really posh, but if she was she wouldn't be looking to buy a house in the middle of Bogsville – she goes, 'Calm down, Pat. Let's at least look the place over ... we've come this far,' obviously knowing their options in the housing market are limited, which makes them, like, easy prey for me. Of course, I'm there leading them through the gaff – a total dump if I'm honest, which I'm not – going, 'You will have seen on your approach that this is a desirable residence in an exclusive enclave of sumptuously designed houses by an award-winning architect ...' Actually, the award-winning part is a bit cheeky. As JP's old man says, the only thing the goy was ever awarded was temporary release from a four-year sentence for trying to bribe council officials, roysh, though as my desk diary said this morning, You've got to speculate to accumulate ...

I'm going, 'These innovative homes with their well-proportioned living areas, blah blah blah, generous specifications, bullshit bullshit bullshit, possible Section 23 relief, piece of focking cake.' The goy mutters something about the TSB/ESRI house price index, whatever the fock that is, and the impending national spatial strategy – again, he's on his own there – and I just go, 'With the market in a state of flux, any theory I might postulate is as good as the next man's,' which is the emergency line to bluff your way out of any difficult corner in this job, and he just nods his head, roysh, and seems to accept what I've said.

I know what's coming next. Of course it's Emma Forbes who asks. She's like, 'Are you prepared to be flexible on the price?' I'm like, '*I* am. Unfortunately, though, the market isn't as generous as me. I have to remind you that I have two other clients to show around this afternoon.' The two of them stand there humming and hawing, roysh, while I'm hitting them with things like, 'optional full furniture fit-out package', 'rear-facing garden with sunny aspect', and other bullshit, knowing damn well the saps aren't going to get anything better than this. The goy's like, 'Okay, we'll offer the asking price. What is it, €210,000?' I'm there, 'Excellent,' showing them out. I go, 'Now, unfortunately, there are two other clients coming this afternoon. It's the highest offer I'm obliged to take, you understand that.' They both nod, looking all mopey, roysh, like someone pissed on their corn-flakes.

I actually don't have anyone else coming to see the house, but I thought I'd let the fockers sweat. I wait around in my cor for about twenty minutes, let them get a good head stort on me, roysh, then I hit the strategic radial corridor back to Dublin.

* * *

During the summer, roysh, I was stringing along these two birds, we're talking Becky and Iseult, and in the heat of the moment, roysh, I told both of them that I'd fallen in love with them, basically just trying to get my bit out of them. This is not actually unusual for me, roysh. I've been known to play five or six girls together at the same time, hence the Little Richard nickname that's mentioned on the back of one of the cubicle doors in the men's in Annabel's.

What made this one different, roysh, was the fact that Iseult and Becky were actually in the same class at school, we're talking sixth-year Whores on the Shore here, and keeping them apart was basically a tightrope act, which I have to say I managed to perform pretty well, until the day they both asked me to the same debs.

The goys were giving me total slaggings, roysh, telling me I'm getting far too old for that whole lark, and I did say that last year's Mount Anything debs would be my last – the chicken à la crème was the best-looking bird there – but I love, like, defying the odds, roysh, and the challenge of bringing two birds to the one debs, without them actually knowing about each other, was enough to persuade me out of retirement for one night only. Fionn turns around to me in the gaff one night and he goes, 'Never been done before, Ross.' I'm like, 'Odds?' He goes, 'We're talking 25 to 1.' I'm like, 'I'm up for the challenge.'

Day arrives, roysh, and I grab a hundred bills from the Drinklink, hit Blackrock, grab two orchids and two boxes of Leonidas chocolates, the medium-sized box, no point in going mental as I've been there and back with both of them. I get back to the gaff, roysh, and I phone up Iseult first and she's like, 'Of all the people I could be going with tonight, I'm SO glad it's you, Ross. You have been SO good for me, especially when I didn't get the points to do international commerce with German,' and eventually, roysh, after I've finished borfing, she asks me to call up to her gaff – this huge pad in Glenageary – at, like, six o'clock because her parents are having, like, a cocktail porty beforehand, which is music to my ears because Becky doesn't want me to pick her up until eight, so I've got time to play with.

Iseult's old pair are just like Iseult, saps basically, giving it the whole, 'So, this is the young man Iseult has spent the *entire* summer talking about,' bit, roysh, and Iseult's like, 'OH! MY! GOD! Daddy, you are SO embarrassing me,' and I'm there going, you can focking cut that out right now, because they've basically got me down as, like, future son-in-law material here. It's all, like, bullshit talk for about half an hour, roysh, me knocking back Diet Cokes and losing the will to live.

Eventually, we head off and I drop Iseult off at the Shelbourne, roysh, then tell her I've forgotten to bring this amazing present I bought her (she's like, 'Oh, you are SO sweet') and I hop back in the cor and peg it out to Becky's gaff in Stillorgan. Oh my God, roysh, Becky's old pair have invited half the focking world around for drinks, we're talking aunts, uncles, neighbours, you name it. Her old man is a total dickhead, leading me around the sitting room, roysh, with his arm around my shoulder, introducing me to all his, I don't know, business associates I suppose, going, 'This is Ross, Rebecca's boyfriend,' which is news to me, though I say nothing. He goes, 'Captained Castlerock the year they won the Cup, 1999 I think I'm right in saying.'

Her old dear, who was actually a bit of a yummy-mummy, spent the next, like, half an hour practically force-feeding me focking vol-au-vents before we finally escaped with a few words of treat-my-daughter-like-a-princess advice from the penis in the Pringle sweater. I'm like, 'Your parents are really cool,' as we get in the cor. She goes, 'I'm SO glad you got on well with them.'

The trickiest part of the evening, roysh, was the meal, the big dilemma being who do I sit with. Basically what I did, roysh, was

I asked Iseult would she mind if I sat at another table, just for, like, the meal and shit. She goes, 'Oh my God, you don't want to be seen with me? Is it, like, the dress?' I'm like, 'No, no, I just want to have a chat with Hayser' – this goy who was at school with me – 'he's pretty upset about not making the UCD team this season.' She looks at me and then at Hayser, roysh, then she goes, 'Oh my God, you are SO a good friend,' and she gives me this, like, peck on the cheek, roysh, and I just fock off.

So there I am, roysh, sat at a table across the far side of the room, with Hayser on one side of me and Becky on the other, and I nearly choke on a garlic and cheese potato when Becky turns around to me at one stage and goes, 'OH! MY! GOD! Iseult Mooney must have come on her own. What a sad bitch.' I'm basically there coughing and spluttering my guts up. I'm like, 'Who's Iseult Mooney?' still trying to play it cool as a fish's fart. She goes, 'Oh, believe me, she is not someone you'd want to know.' I'm like, 'Well, I'm glad I'm here with you and not her,' and she looks at me and goes, 'Oh my God, this is turning out to be SO one of the best nights of my life.'

It was the perfect crime, roysh. After the meal, it was, like, twenty minutes with one, then the other, back and forth all night, the two birds thinking I was their date for the night, and I was sitting there, roysh, storting to let my guard down, pretty confident at that stage that I was even going to end up scoring the two of them at the end of the night, but then it just, like, totally came apart, and we're talking TOTALLY here.

I completely forgot, roysh, but this bird, Aoibheann, let's just say a very recent conquest who I might also have said the dreaded L-word to, she was there as well, roysh, and she ends up getting completely off her face, having a row with me over what a bastard I am to women and then focking a vodka and Red Bull over me. Of course, Iseult and Becky arrive over at exactly the same time and they both want to know – 'OH MY GOD! OH MY GOD! OH MY GOD!' – what's going on. And that's when they find out about, well, each other. Becky goes to Aoibheann, 'That's, like, my boyfriend,' and Iseult turns around to Becky and she's like, '*Hello*? You're, like, delusional, girl.'

Aoibheann sort of, like, disappears, roysh, and the two birds are left there, like, screaming at each other. I'm not sure if they've, like, copped on what's been going on here tonight, but it's obvious they've been dying to get stuck into each other for a while. Becky tells Iseult that Iseult has SO had it in for her ever since she took her place on the hockey team, and Iseult tells Becky she's a knob, always was and always will be. She goes, 'You were always SO up Miss Pendleton's orse.' Becky tells Iseult she has an attitude problem – a TOTAL attitude problem, she goes – and, flattering as it is, roysh, to have two birds fighting over me, I decide then to get the fock out of there when no one is looking. I was just like, 'Goodnight, Vienna.'

CHAPTER SIX
The One Where Ross Has A Cunning Plan

I'm in the newsagents, roysh, the one around the corner from the old pair's gaff, and the queue's, like, out the focking door, and I'm just there flicking through the magazines, waiting for them all to clear out, but the owner, roysh, he's blabbing away to some old dear about the euro and whether we'll ever, like, get used to it, and I'm there thinking what a mutt Patsy Kensit is without make-up and that Patsy Palmer isn't much better, with or without, when all of a sudden, roysh, I hear the goy go, 'You know that magazine's for women,' which is when I realise, roysh, that the shop's empty, at long focking last.

I head up to the counter, roysh, and the goy goes, 'Oh it's you, Ross. Didn't recognise you there. It's the baseball cap. You're not wearing one today.' Then he goes, 'And Charles, how the hell is he?' It never ceases to amaze me how easily taken in people are by that dickhead. I'm like, 'My dad's the same as ever,' and I wonder whether he heard what I actually said because he storts breaking his shite laughing – we're talking, like, really over the top laughing – and slapping the counter, and when he's finished, roysh, he goes, 'That's him alright. That's our Charles.'

I'm just staring at the goy, roysh, and eventually, when he

calms down, I'm like, 'Do you sell *The Star*? It's a newspaper.' He goes, 'I do, for my sins. It's over there, bottom shelf, next to the manila envelopes and the shiny wrapping paper.' I'm like, 'How many copies do you get in?' He's like, 'Em … ten, I think.' I'm like, 'You get in ten copies every day.' He goes, 'Well, it was very popular there during the summer. When the World Cup was on … what's all this about, Ross?' I'm like, 'I want them. I mean I want to buy them. All of them. All ten.' He looks at me, roysh, squinting his eyes, and he goes, 'You're not in some kind of trouble, are you? There's not something in there you don't want your mum and dad to read, is there?'

Before I can say no, roysh, he grabs a copy and lashes it out on the counter and he storts, like, opening pages at random and reading the headlines, going, '**JORDAN TO GIVE BIRTH ON THE INTERNET!** It wasn't you, Ross, was it? You didn't impregnate the buxom, attention-seeking glamour model, did you? Did you?' Holy fock, I knew the goy was, like, weird, but I didn't know how weird. I'm like, '*What* are you bullshitting on about?' He goes, '**WEE WILLY WIMPY! POP IDOL OPENS HIS HEART ON SCHOOL BULLIES WHO MADE HIS LIFE HELL!** You didn't, Ross? You didn't steal lunch money from television's monkey-faced warbler, maybe stick his head down the toilet? Oh, for the love of humanity. **"MAN WHO SAID S**T IN FRONT OF MY KIDS MADE ME MAD! I COULD HAVE PUNCHED HIM ON THE NOSE," SAYS RONAN!** This is the one, isn't it, Ross? You made nice guy Ronan lose his legendary cool by using the S-word in front of baby Jack. It's no wonder you don't want your parents reading this. Can you live with it, Ross? Can you live with yourself?'

I'm like, 'Sorry, will you shut the fock up for a minute. It's got nothing to do with any of that shit. I want to buy all your copies of *The Star*. Not just today. *Every* day. And I don't want you ordering more. That's the deal. You put the ten copies aside for me and anyone else asks you for it you tell them it's sold out.' I pull out a wad of notes and slap five euros down on the counter. I'm like, 'There's plenty more where that came from.' He goes, 'Well there'd want to be. Sure, that wouldn't even cover the cost of the papers.' Focking Monopoly money. I slap a twenty down on top of it. I'm like, 'There's twenty-five euros in it for you, then. We're talking every day here.' He goes, 'Fine.'

My phone beeps. Text message from Sorcha. She wants me to go out with her tonight for, like, something to eat and shit. She's home from Australia for a week for the opening of her old dear's new shop in the Powerscourt Townhouse Centre. She's going back tomorrow and I still haven't seen her. I'll text her later. I'm like, 'Do you also stock the *Herald*?' He goes, 'The Hedild? Yes, it's an evening newspaper. We get about twenty of those in. Very popular.' I'm like, 'I'll take them. All twenty. Same deal. You take the bundle in, you stick it under the counter, and if anyone asks, you tell them it's sold out.' He goes, 'And do you want me to have all these papers delivered to the house?' I'm like, 'No, burn them. Do you have anywhere you can do that?' He goes, 'I've an old barrel in the yard out the back.' I'm like, 'There you are. And let's call it a nice round fifty-five euros a day for the lot. And I don't want to see either of those two newspapers selling in this shop again. Got it?'

He nods, roysh, and he's like, 'I'm with you now, Ross.' I slap another thirty bills on the counter, roysh, and I go and gather up the bundle of Hedilds and tell him to get that fire storted. He looks really sad. I'm like, 'What's your problem?' He's like, 'I love the papers, Ross. It's the scandal, you see. I love the scandal.' I throw my eyes up to heaven, roysh, I'm basically too soft really, then I pull one of the papers out of the bundle and I hand it to him. I'm like, 'Go on then, you can have one last read.' He's all delighted with himself. He, like, scans the front page, roysh, and he goes, '**LAWLOR'S CELLMATE SPEAKS**,' and as I'm heading out the door, he calls me and when I turn around he goes, 'Oh, Ross, you're not Liam Lawlor, are you? Your father would be so disappointed.'

I get outside the shop, hop into the cor, and I ring the old man. I'm like, 'You know some focking weirdos.' He goes, 'Hey, Kicker, how are you?' I'm like, 'Less of the focking old pal's act. That goy in the shop near the gaff ...' He goes, 'Frank? He's a bit much at times, yes, but he means well. Anyway, listen to me, Ross, we've more important things to discuss. You should see what's arrived next door.' I'm like, 'What?' He goes, 'A caravan. A *caravan*, if you don't mind.' I'm like, 'So? Maybe they're planning to go away on holidays.' He goes, 'We did not buy a house in Foxrock so we could end up living next to a bloody ... HALTING SITE.' I'm like, 'Chill out, will you?' He goes, 'I will NOT chill out. And what about that little job I gave you. Two months I gave you to get them out. Two weeks have already gone and still no sign.' I'm like, 'What do you think I was doing at the newsagents?' And there's, like, silence on the other end for about ten seconds, like it's slowly dawning on him. He goes, 'Damn it, you're up to something.' I'm like, 'You're damn right I'm up to something. I'm smoking them out. Smoking them out.'

✱ ✱ ✱

Michelle from Ulster Bank has noticed that I don't have a

pension. She leaves a message on my mobile reminding me that the current State pension is basically only one hundred and thirteen euros a week, which isn't a lot, she says, when you consider that the average industrial wage is, like, three hundred and eighty euros a week. She says that pensions offer substantial growth on your investment and are the only form of regular saving that offers you tax relief, blah blah focking blah.

✳ ✳ ✳

Sorcha orders a raw salad and, like, a bottle of Evian – some things never change – then takes out her Marlboro Lights and puts them on the table. I'm there, 'How's knobhead?' cracking on that I don't know the goy's name, roysh. She's like, 'You're talking about Killian, I take it?' I'm like, '*What*ever. Where is he?' She goes, 'He's in Australia. I know what you're getting at, Ross, and you're wrong. We *actually* have a very healthy relationship, if you must know.' I'm like, 'Meaning?' She goes, 'Meaning we both like our freedom. Meaning we don't have to be full-on, twenty-four seven.' Meaning Killian's got another Sheila on the go by the sounds of it. I decide not to push it, though.

She changes the subject, asks me how Christian is. I'm like, 'We're back talking again after … well, you know.' She's like, 'Are his mum and dad back together?' and I go, 'No, but … they didn't break up over me, you know.' She ignores this and tells me she's sorry she didn't get to see all the goys, but it was really only a flying visit and there was so much, like, family stuff to do. I ask her what time her flight is tomorrow, roysh, and she says ten o'clock and when I tell her, roysh, that I'd like to go to the airport to see her off, she goes, 'Much as I'd *like* to buy that attractive piece of merchandise, somehow it doesn't fit,' which sounds suspiciously like another line from 'Dawson's Creek', and she takes off her scrunchy, slips it onto her wrist, shakes her hair free, puts it back in the scrunchy and then pulls a few strands free. Like I said, some things never change.

Her raw salad arrives. So does my yasai itameru. My phone rings when we're, like, halfway through our food and it's the old man, having an eppo as per focking usual. He's like, 'Ross, come quickly. *He's* been here, Ross.' I'm like, 'Whoa! Whoa! Whoa! Who's *he*?' He goes, '*Him*, Ross. Him next door. Called here about five minutes ago. Brazen as you like. With a ladder. "Couldn't help but notice there's a couple of slates missing off yisser roof," he said. Trying to get money out of me. The gall of it! Oh, if I'd had my wits about me, of course, I'd have hit him with something hard, but my golf bag was just out of reach and, well, it's the shock, you see. And he must have seen it in my face, because he said, "I told herself the day we won the lorro, money or no money, I'm carrying on working. You'd go off yisser head otherwise, Charlie." He called me Charlie, Ross. CHARLIE!' I'm like, 'Hey, I need you focking calm. Stay with me here. What did you do next?' He goes, 'I slammed the door in his face.' I'm like, 'Good.' He's there, 'And I'm just about to call the Gardaí.' I'm like, 'Do NOT call the feds. I mean it. I am handling the situation. I pulled off a focking masterstroke today. Another week and they'll be gone, I'm telling you.' I manage to talk him down and then I hang up.

There's this old dear, roysh, suddenly standing over our table and she's with, like, her daughter I presume, pretty tasty, nice boat race, Ashley Judd with blonde hair, and this complete toss-pot who I reckon is her daughter's boyfriend from the way they're holding hands. Anyway, roysh, this old dear goes, at the top of her voice, 'ARE YOU TWO GOING TO BE

FINISHED SOON?' And Sorcha, roysh, who's been, like, chasing this water chestnut around her plate with her fork for the past ten minutes, she looks up and she goes, 'We are *trying* to have our lunch. Do you mind?' And the three of them, roysh, they're totally focking bulling it, but they don't fock off, roysh, they just stand over us, thinking it'll make us leave quicker.

Sorcha's, like, trying to ignore them and she goes, 'Where were we? You're working for your dad now?' I'm like, 'Yeah, just a one-off thing. I'm still working for JP's old man, in the estate agents. But my old man asked me to do, em, a special project, you could call it.' She goes, 'Is it my imagination or are our horizons unexpectedly broadening?' Her and that focking programme. I'm just like, 'Yeah, Kool and the Gang.' She goes, 'So what exactly does this special project involve?' I'm like, 'Well, tomorrow morning I'm going to offer the goy in the off-licence two hundred bills to stop selling Linden Village and Dutch Gold.' She goes, 'Dutch what?' I'm like, 'Dutch Gold. It's beer. Central heating for skangers.' She's about to light her cigarette, but stops when she hears this, the flame about an inch away from the end of it, and she's there, 'Why would you want to pay the local off-licence to stop selling it?' I'm like, 'Long story. Suffice it to say that the old pair have got some Tallafornian refugees living next door. And you could say their application for asylum has been revoked.' I don't know where that last bit came from, but I have to say, roysh, I'm pretty happy with it.

Sorcha's not. She goes, 'Oh my God, you are *such* a materialistic snob.' I just, like, shrug my shoulders and I'm there, 'How much did that shirt cost?' She goes, 'Oh, so you can't wear Abercrombie *and* be concerned about those less fortunate than you, is that what you're saying? Don't go there, Ross. Do *not* go there.'

All of a sudden, roysh, I notice that the old biddy who was trying to get us to leave has collared one of the waitresses, roysh, and she's going, 'I mean, could they not move to that table over there? They could share with that couple. We need three seats, you see.' But the waitress, roysh, she hasn't a focking clue what your one is talking about and then Sorcha makes a big deal of ordering, I don't know, a grande orange mocha-chip frappuccino or some shite, with extra chocolate as well, and the old bitch, roysh, she throws her eyes up to heaven and then hops it before I have to tell her to.

Sorcha goes, 'That's one thing I can't get used to. Ireland has changed SO much.' I'm like, 'You've only been away eight months,' and she goes, 'Will you share a bowl of chunky dairy peach ice cream with me?' and I know the thing'll come, roysh, and she'll basically horse the lot. That's birds for you. They don't want to share the ice cream. They want to share the guilt. I'm like, 'Okay.' She orders, roysh, then she goes, 'Dublin especially has SO changed. Totally. Everyone is, like, SO rude. Nobody cares about other people anymore, it's all, like, money, money, money.' I remind her that Philipa was saying the same thing six months ago. Philipa as in Shut Sellafield. Philipa as in Save the focking Dolphins. The last time I saw her she was working in some morkeshing firm, blabbing on about consumer recognition, aural spillover and the glamour-sex-excitement curve. You'd need a focking degree in bullshit to understand her. When I say this, roysh, Sorcha suddenly looks all sad. She goes, 'I used to love that Labi Siffre song, 'Something Inside so Strong'.' I reach across the table, roysh, grab her hand and I go, 'I remember, Sorcha. It was one of the main reasons you joined Amnesty.' She goes, 'I come home, I turn on the television and it's on an ad for a bank.' I tell her I've missed her. She ignores me, pulls her hand away and says that Philipa is a sap who always had an attitude problem. Then she storts looking around to see what's keeping her coffee. She looks great.

✳ ✳ ✳

I meet Faye in Dun Laoghaire and she has, like, a bag with her and I ask her whether she's been to the gym. She goes, 'Just for a sauna. And a sunbed. Did you hear about Amy?' I'm there, 'Em, about her joining Riverview?' And she stares through me and goes, 'That girl is *such* a sad case.'

✳ ✳ ✳

For the past three weeks, I've been seeing this bird called Eimear, roysh, well-stacked, nice boat race, but basically thicker than the queue outside a northside post office on family allowance day. Which doesn't matter to me, of course. To me, it's only a bit of fun. The problem is that she's, like, totally fallen head-over-heels for me, the sappy bitch. I haven't mentioned it yet, roysh, but Eimear has a boyfriend, which seems to be a problem to her. I couldn't give a fock. To me, roysh, birds with boyfriends are the best kind of birds to be with. Playing off the big striker, we call it. He takes all the knocks, the elbows and the rough treatment, while you do all the scoring. The last few weeks, roysh, I've been like that Robbie Keane. Without the jewellery, though. And the Tallaght accent.

Eimear and Michael – that's the boyfriend, roysh, or Big Quinny, as the goys christened him – they live in this gaff down near Dun Laoghaire Dorsh station, a bit of a hovel if the truth be told, but pretty much what you'd expect for, like, students. I don't really listen to her that much, roysh, but he's doing, like, veterinary science in Trinity, which takes serious brains, and she's doing, like, commerce in UCD, which doesn't.

But it's obviously not brains she's after, roysh, because last Friday she, like, texts me to tell me that Michael's in Wexford for the weekend, I don't know, shoving his arm up cow's orses or whatever it is vets do, and she's like, **WOOD U LIKE 2 COME 4 DNNER?** and you know me, I'm like, *Hello*? Is the bear a Catholic? Does the Pope shit in the woods?

Lash on my black DKNY shirt and my Hugo Boss jeans, quick splash of *Gio Acqua Di*, and the next thing I know I'm in her sitting room, taking in the smell of some chickeny thing she's cooking while flicking through her CD collection for one bad enough to Petty Pilfer. She's giving it, 'Oh my God, I am such a bad cook. I'm, like, SO embarrassed.' As it turns out, of course, she's not. The nosebag is amazing and when we've finished eating, roysh, we – as Fionn says – retire to the drawing room for the preliminaries.

She's another one of those birds who love that whole oh-romance-me thing, roysh, which is why I agreed to sit with her through the whole of *Sleepless in Seattle*, which is basically the biggest pile of shite ever to be made into a film. By the time it's over, roysh, I'm totally gagging for it, but she wants to put on *Dirty Dancing*. I'm like, 'I'm, em, a bit tired … Eimear.' I nearly called her Orla. I'm like, 'I think I'll turn in.' She goes, 'Nobody puts Baby in the corner,' which I think is a line from *Dirty Dancing*, then she storts breaking her shite laughing, which is when I realise she's either drunker or thicker than I thought.

We head through to the bedroom, all lava lamps and three-bar electric heaters, which is pretty much what you'd expect from a girl you met in Club M. I whip the threads off, roysh, but by the time I get into the scratcher, roysh, she's out for the count and snoring her focking head off, so I climb into the sack, as clumsy as I can, to try to, like, wake her up, but it's no go, and now I know I shouldn't have let her open that second bottle of wine.

I'm in a bit of a Pauline Fowler at this stage, but you don't score as many birds as I have in my life, roysh, without learning a trick or six. I already knew my next move. Okay, I'm lying there, wide awake and basically dying for it, roysh, and she's lying there, out to the world and basically not dying for it, so I grab her by the shoulders, roysh, and I stort, like, shaking her, and just as she's waking up, roysh, I'm there going, 'It's okay, Eimear … ssshh … calm down … it's okay, you just had a bad dream.'

Of course, she wakes up and she's totally clueless. She's like, 'What's wrong?' I'm like, 'You were having a nightmare.' She's there, 'Was I?' I'm like, 'Yeah. That's all it was, a bad dream.' Of course, in her half-asleep state, roysh, she's convinced now that she *was* having a nightmare and she storts, like, crying, which is when I offer her a comforting hug and, well, I don't need to draw you a map of where we're going next.

Or rather, where we *should* have been going next. There's me and Eimear about to get jiggy, roysh, when all of a sudden I hear the door of the flat open and Eimear's like, 'That's Michael. Are you ready for this?' I'm like, 'I thought you said he was in Wexford.' She goes, 'Ross, we have to stop all this sneaking around. He needs to know.' There's no time for me to, like, argue and shit. In he comes and asks that stupid question I've heard so many times before: 'What's going on here?' The state of him, he's a total bogger, I mean, who dressed him – Stevie Wonder? Eimear goes, 'I'm sorry you had to find out this way, Michael. But … we love each other.' I'm like, Whoah, horsey. Who said anything about … This goy, Michael, he goes, 'What's your name?' I'm like, 'What's it to you?' He's there, 'Well, you've eaten all my food, drunk all my wine and now you're sleeping with my girl-friend in my bed. I'm just curious.' Good comeback, I have to give him that. I'm like, 'The name's Ross.'

He goes, 'Outside. Now.' Eimear's there, 'Please, no fight-ing,' I'm like, as *if*. He's only a little goy, roysh, and I'm pretty confident of decking the focker. I hop out of bed and I see him clock my pecs. It turns out, roysh, he doesn't want to fight. It's really weird, roysh, but we go into the kitchen and he tells me to sit at the table, then he pours, like, two large glasses of whiskey. He takes a sip of his and goes, 'Did you know that Eimear hates Christmas?' I'm like, 'What's that got to do with the price of cabbage?' He goes, 'She hates Christmas and she's allergic to milk and she can't swim. And she loves pigs and she cries when she hears Karen Carpenter sing 'Solitaire'. And she's a diabetic and she wants to be a concert pianist and she once dyed her hair blonde and it turned bright orange. And her mum died when she was three.' This is, like, weird shit. He's like, 'And *you* don't know anything about her, do you?' I'm just like, 'No.' He goes, 'And you say you love her?' I'm there, 'Fock, no, *she* said that, not me.'

And suddenly, she's at the door of the kitchen, roysh, and she's like, 'Ross?' And I just knock back the whiskey in one go and I get up from the table, and she's there going, 'Ross? Ross, this isn't fair.' I stop and I look at her and I'm like, 'Nor is Saman-tha Mumba's orse.' It's a JP line – one of his better ones – and I tell them I'll let myself out.

I hear them crying, talking, trying to put what they had back together, as I sneak into the sitting room on my way out the door, roysh, and grab the Phil Collins *Buster* soundtrack that will be my little souvenir of one majorly focked-up night.

✱ ✱ ✱

'I've been watching 'Fair City' for ten years,' Fionn goes, while cleaning his glasses on his shirt. 'It's supposed to be a slice of authentic north Dublin life. Yet in all that time I've never seen anyone being held up with a syringe. Explain that.' I'm like, 'I can't. Come on, Fionn, you can watch the omnibus. We're heading out.' I was *so* gagging to go on the rip, roysh, just to, like, celebrate making my twenty-fifth house sale that morning. It turned out basically to be a piece of piss. Even got out to the gaff half an hour late, roysh, traffic was the usual focking mare, and the goy and the bird are waiting outside in the rain, her looking at her watch and, like, throwing her eyes up to heaven, roysh, to try to make me feel bad. She's like, 'About time, too.' And before I can say a word, roysh, she goes, 'Now, talk to us like we're children. Sell us the house, but spare us the bloody jargon, okay?'

I'm like, 'Hey, Kool and the Gang,' roysh, and then I stort, like, showing them around, basically just spouting bullshit. I'm there, 'This little baby is the last word in top-end, high-spec houses. It's far more than just a location, you might almost say it's a new way of living. It affords generous living space, having been substantially extended over recent years, sometimes with planning permission. Generous electrical specification in every room, concrete driveway, a high-quality fit-out kitchen. It's got SFCH, WC, GDP, ESP and TV3 …'

The bird, roysh, a real nosy bitch, she goes, 'Does it have DG?' I'm like, 'D-what?' And she throws her eyes up to heaven again and goes, 'DG! Double glazing! The house is on a main road, I imagine it's very noisy.' I'm there, 'Extensive public road front-age is one of the features that makes this house so desirable. Some might consider the noise a downside, so all of the windows are, em, DG-able. But can I just encourage you to take a helicop-ter view of the situation. House price inflation may have reduced the affordability of houses in the city, but Ballyboden, sorry Dundrum, is proof that there's still room in the city for the more discerning buyer. Sales activity in this area means you can expect excellent capital appreciation.'

The goy's, like, scratching his head. He goes, 'I thought the market had slowed ...' I'm like, 'You'd think that global economic uncertainty would impact on consumer confidence, but the sluggishness in activity that was evident in the first half of the year hasn't continued into the second half. It really is the time to buy.' This bird, roysh, she goes, 'We thought it was the time to sell.' And I just look at her, roysh, full of, like, pity, and I go, '*Who* told you that?' She's there, 'Your boss did. When he told us to put our house on the market last week.' Fock him. I'm like, 'Em, well, yes, of course it's time to sell. But at the same time, it's also time to buy. It's time to sell and then buy, you might say. It's a seller's-then-buyer's market.'

The bird, roysh, I'm really getting sick of her now, she goes, 'Why is the house called Beachview?' I'm like, 'Well, if you go into the master bedroom ...' She goes, 'The master bedroom is west-facing. The nearest beach is Galway. Comes with a tele-scope, does it?' I'm like, 'Sorry, I meant the box room.' Of course she had to go and check it out, roysh, so we all had to, like, traipse all the way up the focking stairs again and we're all staring out the window at the back of the house and she's still not happy. She's like, 'Well, *I* can't see the sea.'

I'm trying not to lose my rag with her. I'm there, 'You can just make it out. Between the graveyard and the tyre factory there.' She goes, 'That's a drop of rain on the window.' I'm like, 'Oh. Actually, when they said Beachview, I think they meant the tree.' The bird goes, 'You mean the one that's blocking out the natural light in the sitting room?' Fock it, I'm losing them. I'm like, 'Yeah. They're all in this year. Beech is the new, I don't know, oak.'

The goy, roysh, who's actually sound, he goes, 'That type of beech has two Es.' And I'm like, 'A bit like me in English. An E in the Junior Cert and an E in the Leaving,' and he cracks his shite laughing. I'm like, 'Sorry, spelling's never been my strongest point. I was on the S at school,' and the goy's ears prick up, roysh, and he's, like, all of a sudden all interested. He goes, 'What school did you go to? Good God, you're not Gick, are you?' and I'm there, 'No, I went to, em ...' and I'm there trying to guess where the goy went to, roysh. He looks really loaded, roysh, but a bit focking dim, so I go, 'Clongowes,' and all of a sudden he high-fives me and then launches into this, like, song about, I don't know, honour and glory, and I just smile and do this sort of, like, conducting motion with my hands, knowing that the house was as good as sold.

CHAPTER SEVEN
The One Where Ross Does A Shitty Thing

I'm locked, roysh, and I end up trying to make a move on Erika. Of course, I crash and burn. As usual. She goes, 'The gap is too big, Ross.' I'm like, '*Hello?* I'm only a year older than you.' She goes, 'I'm talking about the one between your ears,' and everyone breaks their shites laughing. I'm like, 'Very funny.'

✳ ✳ ✳

Cara is this bird we used to know when we were all, like, fifteen or sixteen and hanging around in McDonald's in Blackrock, eight of us sitting around one caramel sundae. She was a bit of a honey, roysh, but she never actually ended up being with any of us, just basically flirted her orse off. Flirted her orse off and hung around the Frascati Centre all day, which is how she got the nickname The Mall Teaser.

It was a total shock to me to find out a couple of weeks ago, roysh, that she's suddenly going out with Oisinn, having presumed for all these years that she was either a lezzer or was saving herself for Matt Damon. And Oisinn's no Matt Damon, that's for sure, the fat focker, and he generally goes for fat, ugly mingers.

Anyway, roysh, there I am a while back sitting up at the bor in the Wicked Wolf, getting into this really heavy conversation with Fionn about relationships and shit. Basically what happened was that I got, like, a letter from Sorcha that morning. I knew it was from her before I even opened it because on the envelope it had: *The paper used in the manufacture of this product comes from a sustainable forest source.* It turns out anyway, roysh, that her and Dick-Features split up, like, permanently when she went back to Australia and she's basically trying to suss me out to see whether she's any chance of getting back in with me when she comes home after Christmas. It's full of, like, hints, her asking me whether I'm seeing anyone special at the moment, blah blah blah.

I've no real interest in getting back with her at this moment in time, roysh – without wanting to sound like a total asshole, I just want to prove to myself that I could have her if I wanted her – but I make the mistake of asking Fionn what he thinks of the idea. Of course, Fionn uses it to launch into his latest theory, which is that no male-female relationship truly lasts more than two years. I'm like, 'Two years? What are you talking about?'

He goes, 'We're apes, Ross,' and I'm like, 'You mean rugby players?' He shakes his head and goes, 'Humans in general. We're one of eighty-nine different species of ape. And apes aren't monogamous.' I'm like, 'This is total bullshit. And we're talking TOTAL here.' He goes, 'Ross, I'm the only friend you have who's still enjoying the benefits of a third-level education. That makes what I have to say even more precious.' I'm like, 'Sorry.' He goes, 'I'm passing on wisdom here, Ross. Be grateful. Your average ape will father many offspring during his lifetime, with several different mothers. Not at the same time, of course. We're not talking about Ballyfermot here.'

I'm like, 'What *are* you talking about?' He shakes his head and he goes, 'I'll use the baby voice then. Daddy ape meets mummy ape. They settle down. Baby ape comes along. Daddy ape stays with mummy ape but only until she can cope with baby ape on her own. Then he goes off to find another mummy ape. The whole process takes two years.' I'm like, 'And?' He goes, '*And …* it's the same for humans. Two years, Ross. Then your instinct takes you to the next tree. To try to keep a relationship going for longer than two years, well, it's focking around with nature.'

Anyway, roysh, all of this is basically just background to the story, which is really about Oisinn and this bird, The Mall Teaser. Basically his old pair had been on at him for ages, roysh, asking him all about this bird he was seeing, trying to get him to bring her home to meet them. Of course, Oisinn's like, '*Hello?* Mortification City, Arizona.' So his old pair – they're, like, *such* nosy fockers – they hear him on his mobile arranging to meet Cara in the Wicked Wolf that night.

So what they do, roysh, is they go to Blackrock to some restaurant for a meal and they decide to – we're talking accidentally on purpose, roysh – pop into the Wicked Wolf afterwards for a drink, just to have a scope at the new bird. What they don't know, roysh, is that it's Wet T-Shirt Night. And who's the star of the show? Up there standing on the bar, doing a sexy dance, soaked in water, big tits hanging out. You've guessed it. Oisinn. Then he drags Cara up on the bar as well and storts pouring water over her. His old man is just standing there with his mouth open. His old dear is bawling her eyes out. JP goes over and offers to buy them a drink. I can hardly take my eyes off Oisinn, though. Fionn turns around to me, a real look of, like, satisfaction on his face, and he goes, 'What did I tell you, Ross? Apes.'

✳ ✳ ✳

A very successful weekend of scoring results in the addition of two new CDs to my growing collection. Janet from Rathgar provided Jewel's *Pieces of You* – unbeknownst to her, of course – and Amanda, this bird I met in Lillies who looks a little bit like Vanessa Marcil, weighed in with the soundtrack from *Grease*. Both are equally shit, but at this rate, by Christmas, I'm going to have to stort a second shelf.

✳ ✳ ✳

There's two rabbits on the screen, roysh, and the male one – I think he's called a buck – he sort of, like, sniffs at the female for a second or two and then suddenly the two of them are, like, going at it hammer and tongs, basically doing the business like there's no tomorrow. Anto, a young rabbit of just six weeks, feels his face go all hot and a sudden stiffening in his jeans as David Attenborough's voice fills the lounge, 'Rabbits have ... many litters between ... early spring and late autumn,' he says in that sort of breathless voice of his. 'There are between four ... and six in each litter.'

But Anto is too engrossed in the sight of the two rabbits humping to hear what David Attenborough's saying, or to notice that his old dear is all of a sudden in the room as well. She's like, 'What the ...' and he quickly tries to flick over, roysh, to pretend he was watching 'The Osbournes'. But she storts, like, whacking him around the head with a rolled-up copy of *Woman's Way* and going, 'Ya dorty beggar. Ya dorty little fookin beggar.'

He's, like, trying to protect himself with his forepaws and he's there going, 'Stall the ball, will ye? I was only flickin' through de channels.' She goes, 'Flickin' through de channels me arse. I know what you're after been doin'.'

His old man comes in then, roysh, and he's like, 'What's the story?' and the old dear goes, 'I'm after catchin' him watchin' one of dem dorty movies ... I can't believe they put that filth on the telly at this hour.' The old man's there, 'A bluey? Is dat all? Moy Jaysus, I thought World War bleedin' Three was after breakin' out.' She's like, '*Is dat all?* What do you mean, *is dat all?* No wonder your son's turned out a bleedin' pervert if that's yer attitude.' He's like, 'Will ye give over, Dolores. Doesn't make him a pervert. The boy's just curious, that's all.' She's like, 'Sex, sex, sex. It's all yous think about.' He's like, 'We're fookin rabbits, for fook's sake. It's nature an' dat.'

The old dear just gives him this filthy, roysh, and she goes, 'I'm not even goin' to tell you what I found under his bed yesterday. It's no wonder I'm buyin' toilet rolls every udder day.' Anto gets a total beamer, roysh, and he goes to get up. His old dear's like, 'Where de fook are you goin'?' He's like, 'To me room.' She's like, 'No, you're not. How long ago was it I asked ye fer to go to the shops?' He's like, 'Ah, Ma.' She's like, 'Up and get me me smokes.' He's like, 'But the shop van's closed now.' She goes, 'Go up to the village then.' He's like, 'At this time? Ma, it's dangerous out there.' The old man's like, 'The boy's right, love. Here, have one of mine.' And she's like, 'I hate fookin John Player, ye know dat.'

He puts his hindlegs up on the table, roysh, grabs the remote control and storts flicking through the channels. He's like, 'Shouldn't be smoking so much in any how. Especially when you're pregnant.' She goes, 'I'm always fookin pregnant. You see to that ... and is it any wonder I'm smokin' so much, raisin' a monster for a son?' The old man suddenly slaps Anto around the side of the head, roysh, and he goes, 'Your mudder's right, don't be watchin' dem pornos.' Anto goes, 'I was only flickin' through de channels.' The old dear's like, 'I'm goin' upstairs, see has Bernie any smokes.'

When she's gone, roysh, the old man storts flicking through the channels again and then he, like, looks at Anto out of the corner of his eye. He's like, 'Which one was it, son?' Anto's like, 'Wha'?' He goes, 'Which one was it?' He's like, 'Em, 'The Livin' Planet, Lagomorpha and Other Burrowin' Mammals'.' The old man's like, 'Ah yeah, one of the lads in the job lent me that before. Happy days ... he's a dorty bastard, that David Attenborough but, isn't he?'

Anto is not yet of an age where he can discuss these things with his old man comfortably. He goes, 'I was only flickin' ...' The old man goes, 'He did anudder one. When he was younger. They all do. 'Life on Earth'. Very hard to get. Animals and everyting in it ... he's a fookin dort burd alright.'

The old dear arrives back, roysh, a lot calmer now she has a cigarette hanging out of her mouth. She's like, 'What's on?' The old man's like, 'Fook-all. Nine o'clock news is just after startin'.' She picks up the *Herald*, roysh, sort of, like, scans the television page for a minute and then, like, grabs the remote off him. She goes, ''The Office Party'. We'll look at that,' and she turns over, roysh, and this, like, elevator music suddenly fills the room and there's this bird, roysh, who's obviously, like, a secretary, and she takes off her glasses and lets down her hair and then she storts, like, doing the business with some bloke, while photocopying various parts of her anatomy and faxing them to the company's office in Cologne.

Anto's like, 'Fook's sake, this is borin'.' The old man thinks so as well, but he doesn't say so, just goes, 'Nothin' borin' about nature, son. A couple of year, you'll be learnin' all this stuff in school.' Anto goes off to his room and lies on his bed, roysh, wonders will he ever meet a doe who likes him – the big question on every six-week-old buck's mind.

And suddenly I wake up, roysh, in a cold sweat, the sheets wringing wet, and when I, like, get my bearings I grab my mobile and, like, ring Christian and I go, 'What the fock was that stuff we were drinking at the porty last night?'

✳ ✳ ✳

Emily, roysh, more a friend than a girlfriend you'd have to say, even though she looks a little bit like Holly Marie Combs and I've been there once, no twice, and even though she's got, like, a boyfriend now, it's a total boost to the old ego to know that I could, like, be with her again if I wanted to, which I'm pretty sure I could. She was on the Mount Anything debating team with Sorcha as well, roysh, and my friendship with her really pisses Sorcha off, which is another reason to, like, keep it going. Anyway, roysh, basically Emily works at her old dear's pet-grooming service and you wouldn't believe this place, we're basically talking a hairdressers for focking dogs here. All these rich old dears come in with these little yappy things growing out of their armpits and they're giving it, 'Please cheer my wittle baby up.' It makes you want to borf, roysh, but these stupid bitches are handing over a hundred bills, no questions asked, to give the dog a cut and blow dry.

Anyway, roysh, this particular day I'm down in Kilpedder of all places showing this couple around a house down there, and on the way back into the office, roysh, I swing by Emily's work to see if she's heading into Lillies on Friday night. I get in there, roysh, and she's like, 'OH! MY! GOD! Ross, you are *such* a lifesaver.' I'm like, 'Why do you say that, babes?' She goes, 'Can you bring that dog out for a walk? Maybe Killiney beach or something,' and I'm like, 'Which dog?' and she points at this big, white, fock-off poodle in the corner, a massive thing, like the one in 'EastEnders', Roly or whatever the fock he was called. It's one of those dogs that looks like it should have four wheels and a handle attached to it to be pushed around by a kid. And Emily must see the reaction on my face, roysh, because she goes, 'Please, Ross. Be a darling.' I'm like, 'If I'm seen walking around with that thing, Emily, people are going to think I've come out. And I couldn't live with hundreds of female suicides on my conscience,' playing it Mister Slick. I'm like, 'Why does he need to go for a walk?' and she's there, 'She, Ross. It's a she. And that's the problem. She's in heat. I've three more dogs booked in this afternoon and I've had to put them out the back. That's what all that barking is.' I'm like, 'But Emily–' and she goes, 'Ross, I'll make it up to you,' and, well, basically I'm a sucker for a hard luck story, especially when it comes from a bird I wouldn't mind knobbing.

So she puts a leash on the focking thing, roysh, and I bring it out to the cor, one hand over my eyes just in case anyone recognises me. I open the boot, roysh, and I go to put her in and Emily's like, 'ROSS!' and I'm there, 'It was a joke. Chill out, will you?' She's like, 'I'm sorry, I am SO stressed out this week. Can't wait for the weekend,' and I put the dog in the passenger seat. She goes, 'Now don't walk her too far, Ross. She has a weak heart,' and I'm like, 'There's no chance of that.' Emily gives me a peck on the cheek and I drive off and the second I get around the corner, roysh, I pull up, take the dog out of the cor and lash her back into the boot.

And as I'm driving along, roysh, I can hear all this whimpering coming out of her and I turn up the CD player – the new Coldplay album – but I can still focking hear it, and I'm storting to lose the rag and I'm there giving it, 'I should just let you loose and let some big dog ride you,' which is when I get an idea, roysh, a brilliant one I have to say. I head for Foxrock, roysh. It's still only two o'clock in the afternoon so the old pair aren't going to be at home. The old man will be at work and the old dear does lunch with the girls from the tennis club on Tuesdays. The traffic's fairly light, roysh, and I get there in no time, I pull up outside the next-door neighbours' house, get out of the cor and have a quick butchers over the fence. They've only moved in a couple of months, roysh, but already they've left their mark on the place, and we're talking big time here. There's, like, mattresses and broken washing machines all over the garden, and spare cor ports and an old fridge and, like, dog shit and black bin bags which have been ripped apart and, like, the rubbish dragged all over the front lawn. Then all of a sudden, roysh – AAARRGGHH! – this growling and borking storts and basically frightens the shit out of me, and I look down, roysh, and it's the knackers' Rottweiler, a big focking angry thing as well, roysh, going basically ballistic it is, and I just thank fock that I'm not on his side of the fence right now. I go to the cor, roysh, open the boot and drag Roly or whatever her name is out. The closer we get, roysh, the more ballistic the Rottweiler gets on the other side of the fence, obviously getting the scent, love is in the air, roysh, but she's, like, really pulling hard against the chain, trying to, like, get away and I have to use all my strength, roysh, to drag her as far as the fence, then pick her up and throw her over it.

All I can hear, roysh, is all this growling and grunting and yelping, and the Rottweiler's either shagging her or eating her, and I'm basically praying it's the first, otherwise this could be a serious test of me and Emily's friendship. It's a couple of minutes before I can, like, even bear to watch, but when I look over the fence again, roysh, the Rottweiler's bet into her, tongue hanging out, eyes rolled into the back of his head and his orse doing ninety, and she doesn't seem to be doing too much complaining either. The next thing, roysh, the trap is sprung. First I hear the back door opening and then I see the goy coming out, roysh, to investigate what all the grunting and groaning is about, and he obviously expects to find the dog doing whatever it is that Rottweiler's do, eating a child or something, but then he sees his killing machine of a dog, roysh, getting his Nat King Cole off a big fluffy poodle and his reaction is basically just what I'd expected.

He just goes, 'TYSON! NOOOOO!' and he runs towards them, roysh, and hits Tyson this almighty focking boot and the two dogs scatter in opposite directions. Then the goy's bird – I think her name's Cindy, roysh – she comes out and she's like, 'What's the story, luv?' and the goy just breaks down in tears and he's like, 'I caught Tyson … shagging a poodle. I mean, shagging a poodle, can you believe it? He's … he's bent. Our dog's a bender.' The bird, roysh, she's like, 'Gays is what dee call dem now. Are ye sure it wasn't a female dog he was ridin'?' and he goes, 'It was a fookin poodle. They're all bleedin' transsexuals, them poodles. Even the men ones look like women.' She's like, 'What're we goin' to do?' and he's there going, 'Might as well ring its neck now. A gay dog's no good to us. I told you, Cindy. What did I tell ye about moving to an area like this? I told ye we'd all go

A. Clarke.

soft. I didn't think Tyson would be the first, though. We should never have left Blanchardstown. A bleedin' gay dog. They don't tell you this kind of thing on the lorro ads, do they?'

The next thing, roysh, the poodle comes leaping over the fence and I grab a hold of her and stick her in the front passenger seat – she deserves to travel in style after what she's been through. Doesn't seem to be much damage, except she's walking a little bit crooked. A nice shampoo and set and no one will be any the wiser, unless of course there's a nasty little shock on the way for her owner in nine months' time, or however long it takes for dogs to have, like, babies and shit.

✴ ✴ ✴

It was a total mare of a weekend, and basically I mean TOTAL. This bouncer turned me away from AKA, roysh, not because I was elephants but because I was, in his words, acting the bollicks at a stag party a few weeks earlier. I'm like, '*Hello?* I don't *think* so. Stag porties are, like, SO working class.' Fionn goes, 'Ross, you must have a dopplegänger.' I'm like, 'A doppelgänger, a Long Island iced tea, I'd drink anything at this stage, Fionn, but this goy won't let me in.'

I think what the problem is, roysh, is that a lot of bouncers are basically jealous of me. They see me in there, roysh, working groups of birds, giving them my lines, getting mobile numbers, basically breaking hearts. It must be a very frustrating job, roysh, fifty notes a night to stand around watching goys like me doing my stuff and going home with whatever bird I want. I'm a good-looking bloke. I've got the chat. I've got the confidence. What do these goys want me to do, sit at home in a coma all night?

The rest of the lads try to persuade him to let me in, roysh, which is the worst thing you can do with bouncers. Christian waves his hand in front of the goy's face and goes, 'You *will* let my friend in,' and the goy goes, 'Listen, pal, any more of that crap and none of you is getting in.' Christian turns around and looks at me, roysh, with this look of, like, disappointment on his face and he goes, 'The goy's a Toydarian. The Force is useless against him.'

I'm like, 'Hey goys, come on, that place is SO focking last year anyway. Let's hit Cocoon.' But Fionn and Oisinn are like, 'No, we'd, em, prefer to go in here. The problem is we're supposed to be meeting people from, er, college in here.' And I can see what's happening, roysh. Basically they know that if I'm off the scene they've a much better chance of scoring. Cuts down the field for them. But what thrill is there in scoring when you know there's no other competition? I'm like, 'Oh, right, so it's a Celtic League night, goys, yeah?' Oisinn just shrugs. I'm like, 'Come on, Christian, we're European Cup players.' But Christian, my so-called best mate, goes, 'Sorry, Padwan, I'm, er, meeting people from college as well.' I'm like, 'You're not even *in* college.' He goes, 'Nor … are they.'

So they all head in, leaving me there like a Toblerone, out on my focking own. I think about heading for the Fightlink, roysh, but I end up hitting Cocoon on my focking sweeney. I sit up at the bor, lorrying back the pints, telling various people who come and stand beside me how, like, difficult it is to be good-looking these days, but most of them just move to the other end of the bor, which is when I realise I'm more trousered than I thought.

Eventually, roysh, I leave and head up Grafton Street to get a Jo Maxi. Miracle of focking miracles, I flag one down on the Green, hop in the back and the goy asks me where I'm going. I'm like, 'Back to my gaff. We're talking Dalkey, roysh.' He's like, 'Eh, sorry, bud. I'm stayin' local.' I'm like, 'Local? Dalkey is ten miles away. How much more local can you get?' He goes, 'When I say local, I mean *local*.' I'm like, 'You're not allowed to do that. You have to take me once I'm in the cor.' He goes, 'I'm not goin' that direction. Look, if you don't get out now, I'll take you straight to the garda station.'

I'm seriously pissed off at this stage, roysh. I'm like, 'Take me to the gorda station. I'm going to make a complaint about you.' So he screeches the focking wheels, roysh, and I must drift off into a drunken sleep or something for a few seconds because the next thing I know, roysh, we're pulling into this cop shop, and there's a cop outside, roysh, and the taxi driver calls him over. We both get out and before I get a chance to say anything, roysh, the driver goes, 'He was being abusive and threatening.'

The gorda, roysh, a focking bogger, you can tell he couldn't give a fock, just wants to get back to his, I don't know, bacon and cabbage or whatever. He's like, 'Do you want me to arrest you?' I'm like, 'Excuse me, I asked him to bring me here to make a complaint. I asked him to take me to Dalkey and he said he was staying local. That's illegal.'

The copper's like, 'Are you trying to tell me the law?' I'm like, 'That *is* the law.' He goes, 'Don't you raise your voice to me.' I'm like, 'I didn't.' He goes, 'You DID raise your voice. I could charge you with assaulting a garda for that.' He winks at the driver, roysh, and the driver heads off back to his taxi, laughing to himself. I stort singing, 'DE-REG-U-LATION. DE-REG-U-LATION. AND WE DON'T HAVE TO QUEUE FOR SIX HOURS TONIGHT,' a song that Oisinn always sings at taxi ranks and which really wrecks the goy's head.

I turn around and the copper's gone, roysh, so I head into the station and demand to see the duty sergeant, which I'd seen the old man do once when he got a ticket for having one wheel on the kerb in Sandycove. You have to give it to the cops in this town, they're really on top of crime. The goy goes, 'The duty sergeant's on his break,' and he slams the hatch shut. I tell him I'll wait.

I sit down beside some goy on this, like, hard chair. The goy's off his face, roysh, and he's got, like, a McGuigan moustache and DUBS tattooed across his knuckles. He smells of piss. I'm like, 'Which Dorsh station do you work in?' He goes, 'I don't work in a Dart station.' I'm like, 'Sorry, it's just a private joke I have.' He goes, 'I used to. Got laid off last week.' I'm like, 'Oh, roysh. What are you waiting for now?' He goes, 'Making a complaint. Police brutality.'

We sit there for, like, half-an-hour and no one comes near us. Eventually, roysh, the goy goes, 'Good night, tonight?' I'm there, 'The worst ever. Don't think just because I'm good-looking that I've no worries.' The goy's too locked to even understand me. I'm there, 'You know, I hate this town. I hate this *focking* town.'

I must be sobering up because I'm storting to wonder what the fock I'm doing still sitting there. I get up and go outside. It's already storting to get bright. I put my hands in the pockets of my chinos and stort walking in the direction of Dalkey.

✷ ✷ ✷

It's half-past five in the morning, roysh, when I pull up outside the old pair's next-door neighbours' gaff and I take out a can of, like, blue spray paint and I write Glasgow Rangers Football Club across the front gate. JP's idea. A nice touch.

✳ ✳ ✳

I did a shitty thing. A really shitty thing. For the last two weeks, all anyone has been talking about is, like, Sophie's liposculpture operation, or I should say rumours about Sophie having a liposculpture operation because basically nobody knew the truth. She told us she was going in to hospital to have, like, an ingrown toenail removed, then said she didn't want any visitors, and the girls were all like, '*Hello*?' and it was actually Aoife who came up with the liposculpture theory on account of the fact that Sophie was always going on about still having a fat chin and fat thighs no matter how much weight she lost.

Chloe goes, 'Why can't she just admit it then? She's spent the last, like, I don't know how many years talking about rhytidectomies and laser skin-resurfacing – the girl is, like, TOTALLY obsessed – and then I asked her what she got for her twenty-first and she couldn't give me a straight answer.' Aoife goes, 'You think it's a rhytidectomy?' I'm like, 'I'm lost. What the fock is a rhytidectomy?' Aoife goes, 'An operation to get rid of, like, sagging skin around your eyes and your lips.' Chloe goes, 'And frown lines. Oh my God, she is going to be *such* a bitch when she gets out of hospital. She's going to think she's SO beautiful.' And Aoife goes, 'She SO will. I bet she makes a move on Simon at Críosa's going-away-to-Australia porty.' Oisinn arrives over with the drinks and he's like, 'Who are you talking about?' and Aoife's like, 'Sophie,' and he goes, 'Did you hear she's having a breast job?' Chloe says she heard it was liposculpture, but Oisinn says it's definitely a breast job because he heard it from Gavin, who's been seeing her sister on and off, say nothing to Katie, we're talking BT2 Katie, because she'd go ballistic. Oisinn goes, 'Definitely boobs. God knows she could do with them.' Aoife's there, 'And a tummy-tuck.' And I tell them I'm going to the bor in a minute if anyone wants a saucer of milk.

All of this is basically background. What happened was, roysh, this particular night, about three days later, I was sitting in the gaff, chilling out, watching the Geri Halliwell yoga video that the goys got me for my birthday, when Oisinn calls over, roysh, and the two of us get talking and somehow we come up with this, like, plan to drive out to the hospital where Sophie's staying, sort of, like, doorstep her, to basically see what she's getting done for ourselves.

I don't want to sound like I'm getting deep here, but you shouldn't, like, judge me, or if you do, roysh, you need to know where I'm, like, coming from. You're talking about a goy whose old dear wrote to the National Gallery to tell them she thought the idea of charging people in to see those new paintings was – and I quote – "splendid, because it deters undesirables from hanging around the place". We're talking about a goy whose old man believes that pound shops are immoral because they – his words now – "exploit the fallen in our society, the unfortunates, the wretched poor". None of this is an excuse for what happened, roysh, but I'm an asshole only because my old pair were assholes before me and it's all to do with, like, genes and shit. So before I tell you the story, you shouldn't judge me.

The cor pulls up outside the hospital and the two of us get out, still breaking our shites laughing, but trying to hold it together long enough to ask the porter what ward she's in. He says St Ann's and we take the stairs two at a time, the adrenaline really going through us now. Oisinn goes, 'This is going to be a laugh,' and I'm like, 'Totally.' This nurse, roysh – black hair, glasses, pretty do-able – she asks us who we're looking for and we tell her and she tells us there's a Sophie in, like, the second last ward on the left. So we head down, roysh, and the room is empty. There's magazines – we're talking *Cosmopolitan*, *Celebrity Spy*, *In Style* – scattered all over the bed, but nothing to show that it's, like, Sophie's ward. I turn around to Oisinn and I go, 'Is that her dressing-gown?' And Oisinn goes, 'How the fock would I know?' I'm like, 'I thought you said you were with her before?' And Oisinn's like, 'Yeah, but she wasn't *wearing* anything obviously.'

All of a sudden, roysh, we turn around and we see her, down the far end of the corridor. She's got her back to us and it's actually her old dear we recognise first. She's standing chatting to her, roysh, so we hang around for, like, a couple of minutes, trying not to look too suspicious, waiting for the old dear to go. After about ten minutes, roysh, she gives Sophie a hug and tells her she'll ring her tonight and then she's, like, gone. Sophie turns around, roysh, and storts, like, walking towards us, holding onto the wall as she does, which is when we notice for the first time, roysh, that her whole face is wrapped in bandages. She's got them, like, around her mouth and over her nose and across her eyes, so she can't see a thing. And as she gets closer, roysh, it's like she's aware of the fact that there's someone standing in front of her because she stops feeling her way down the wall and just stands there. And the look on my face, roysh, it just sets Oisinn off into hysterics. He storts breaking his shite laughing, and Sophie drops this bunch of grapes she's holding. I turn around, roysh, and I go, 'Focking hell, Sophie. You look like the Elephant Man.'

But she doesn't laugh, roysh. She's just there, like, frozen to the spot. And me and Oisinn, roysh, we suddenly hear the sound of, like, water splashing onto the floor. And we look down, and Sophie's, like, pissed herself. Must have been the fright she got. We get the fock out of there before she storts screaming and the nurses call for security. And on the way home not a single word passes between us, between Oisinn and his asshole friend.

CHAPTER EIGHT
The One Where Ross Grows A Heart

Erika says she is *not* putting up with it, she is SO not putting up with it, and she calls over the waitress, roysh, and she goes, 'This soup is cold,' and the waitress, a total focking howiya, she's like, 'I'll change it,' and as she's heading back to the kitchen, Erika goes, 'Hey you.' The chick's like, 'Sorry?' and Erika goes, 'Tell the chef that my sister's a microbiologist. If he spits in that soup, snots in it or anything like that, I'll sue your focking orses. Now go and get me a hot one.' When she's gone, roysh, Erika turns around to Keelin and goes, 'That girl has a *serious* attitude problem. I told you we should have gone to Wagamamma.' Keelin, who's working in, like, human resources, roysh, she tells me that I look SO well in a suit and out of the corner of my eye, roysh, I can see Erika giving her daggers. I wolf down the rest of my tuna and cheese melt and tell them I have to, like, head back to the office, busy afternoon ahead, shitload of paperwork to get through on that house I'm selling, blah blah blah.

I sold this house, roysh – I say house, I mean kennel – we're talking one room downstairs that's, like, big enough for a sofa, a TV, a fridge and a cooker, one bedroom upstairs and a box room big enough to fit a futon. Middle of Drimnagh, called it Crumlin, two hundred grand and the next thing the phone's ringing off the focking hook. Had something like eight offers for the kip. So there's me upping the price all the time. I'm like, 'I'm sorry, we've had a bid of two hundred and ten. You're going to have to upsize your offer if you want to stay in the game.'

And JP's old man, roysh, he's practically frothing at the mouth listening to this, feet up on the desk opposite me, rubbing his big sweaty armpits, going, 'Go on, Ross. Take 'em. Take 'em for five more grand. They've got things they can sell.' So eventually I agree to sell it to this couple, roysh, this real IT wanker and his bird, who said she was, like, a travel agent or some shite, as if I give a fock, they were just making bullshit small talk to try to butter me up when I was showing them around. It was all like, 'It's everything we've ever dreamed of,' and, 'Oh, Tadhg and Arran are SO going to love this room.' I'm just there thinking they'll need a focking shoehorn to get two kids into that room.

They were there, 'If we tighten our belts … don't go out so much … a bit here, a bit there … no more big Christmases for a while …' – I'm there, COME ON! – and then the goy's like, 'Okay, we'll take it.' Two hundred and forty notes they went to. So that was it, roysh, lashed the old Sale Agreed sign on it and left it to the solicitors to, like, I don't know, solicit. So Wednesday afternoon, roysh, the two of them were due to sign for the gaff and, like, one hour before, we're talking one *focking* hour before, we get another offer. The goy who rings up, roysh, he goes, 'How much have you agreed to sell it for?' I'm like, 'Two hundred and fifty.' JP's old man is there egging me on, going, 'Go on, Ross. Go on.' The goy on the phone goes, 'I'll up it to two hundred and fifty-five.' After ten minutes of to-ing and fro-ing, I'm like, 'Sale agreed, my man. Sale agreed.'

Of course, the couple, roysh – Timmons, I think their name was – the two knobs, they try to make me feel bad about it. They ring up, roysh, and the woman's like, 'You didn't show up at the signing.' I'm like, 'I had a better offer.' And she's there, 'Meaning?' getting a bit smart with me. I'm there, 'What I mean is GAME OVER. PLEASE INSERT MORE MONEY,' which I have to say, roysh, I was pretty pleased with. She goes, 'You mean we've been gazzumped?' I'm like, 'Look, I don't know what the Irish for it is and I don't care. All I know is that you're out of the game, and to get back in, you're going to have to come up with another twenty grand.'

JP's old man is in front of me, punching the air, while I'm saying all this to her. She's, like, blubbing her eyes out at this stage. She goes, 'But we've given our notice in the flat we're renting. It's Christmas in two weeks. Where are we going to go?' I'm like, 'We're an estate agents, not a homeless charity,' which is what it says on the sign over JP's old man's desk. 'But ... what are we going to *do*?' she goes. JP's old man, roysh, he must have been through this many times before because he seems to know exactly what this bird is saying. He's shouting, 'They've got kids, haven't they? Get them out earning. Paper round or something.'

She goes, 'My husband doesn't even know I'm ringing. He's gone to see our solicitor.' I'm there, 'Well, if your solicitor is qualified, he'll tell you that no law has been broken. I mean, you could try Marian Finucane, if it's just a sympathetic ear you're looking for.' I'm actually shocked at how easily this stuff is coming to me. JP's old man is dancing around in front of me. I'm like, 'And stop your focking snivelling. You're storting to wreck my head.' She goes, 'We've got two children. What do you suggest I do?' I was SO tempted to say, 'Get yourself sterilised,' roysh, but I didn't. I just went, 'It's going to be another week or two before the other goy signs. Improve your offer.'

When I hang up, roysh, JP's old man is lighting a cigar and just, like, staring at me in admiration. He goes, 'Ross, all my life I've been looking for someone like you. You have no heart and no soul.'

✳ ✳ ✳

I go into Bon Espresso and Patisserie to get a coffee, roysh, and the bird behind the counter goes, 'Black or white?' I'm like, 'Black.' She's about to put the lid on it, roysh, and I'm like, 'Could you put some milk in that as well.' And she goes, 'I thought you said you wanted it black?' I'm like, 'I meant black as in made with water, not milk.' She goes, 'That's not what you said.'

✳ ✳ ✳

Sitting in the gaff in Dalkey, roysh, basically just chilling, watching '90210' and thinking to myself that Tori Spelling actually looks a bit like Shirley Temple Bar, when all of a sudden Erika rings, roysh, and she's like, 'Do you want to head into town? Late-night shopping?' I'm just like, 'Does the Pope shit in the woods?' She tells me she'll pick me up in, like, half an hour and then, before she hangs up, roysh, I hear her going, 'Oh my God, that girl is SO lucky her father is Aaron Spelling.'

Erika's attitude towards me has SO changed in the last few weeks, maybe because she thinks I was with Sorcha when she was home from Australia and now she wants to be with me, roysh, just so she'll have one up on her, which is perfectly alroysh by me. I reckon at this rate I've a pretty decent chance of being with her on Christmas Eve, so even though shopping with birds is basically for knobs, roysh, when she asks me if I wanted to come, I was like, 'Oh yes, I am SO there.' Headed into my room to get ready, roysh, changed back into my work clothes because I know that suits impress her, we're talking my navy Hugo Boss suit and, like, my new blue-and-red sailing jacket, a splash of *Gio Acqua Di*, we're talking the works here.

While I'm lashing the old wax into my hair, roysh, my phone rings and I check caller ID and it's Dick-Features again, so I just let it go to the message-minder. When I play it back, it's like, 'Hello, Ross. Just your old dad here. Your old man, whatever it is you call it. Just ringing with the latest on the pair next door. You won't believe it. Snow spray, Ross! Yep, you heard right. They've written HAPPY XMAS on all the windows in snow spray. Snow spray, thank you very much indeed. Probably taken about twenty thousand euros off the value of our house in the process. The Gardaí were no help, of course. No crime has been committed, etcetera, etcetera. These people know the law inside out. All the loopholes. And the other thing–' Then he suddenly gets cut off. What a knob.

I hear the front doorbell buzzing, roysh, and for one horrible moment I think it might be him, that he's, like, actually managed to find out where I'm living, but it turns out to be Erika, roysh, and she's, like, early. I head downstairs, hop into her cor and go to kiss her on the cheek, but she goes, 'Don't push it,' and then she sort of, like, turns her nose up and goes, '*Gio Acqua Di*? Oh my God, Ross, that is SO last year.' We get into town about seven o'clock, roysh, pork in the Stephen's Green Shopping Centre and head straight for Grafton Street, where there's this big crowd and they're, like, picketing the shop we're heading to, a couple of them I think I recognise from Annabel's, and they're giving out leaflets with **BATTERY BUNNIES** in big writing on them, and they're like, 'Don't go in there, they're selling rabbit fur. Don't go in there, they're selling rabbit fur.'

I stop, roysh, and I'm actually considering not going in, but Erika walks straight past them and I sort of, like, call her back and she turns around and goes, '*Hello*? What is your problem?' I'm like, 'You're not actually going to, like, pass the picket, are you?' She goes, 'Of course I am. There's fock-all in French Connection I like.' One of the protesters, roysh, this fairly alroysh-looking bird who may or may not be Tiernan's cousin, she goes, 'You SO shouldn't go in. Did you not hear what we've been shouting? They're selling rabbit fur in there.' Erika goes, 'And they're selling rabbit stew in Patrick Guilbaud's. So focking what?' And this chick, roysh, the protester one, she goes totally ballistic then, roysh, and we're talking TOTALLY. She's like, 'Oh, so is *that* how you like to think of rabbits, in a stew?' Erika just looks her up and down, roysh, and goes, '*Don't* give me that. I don't even like stew.' And then, just to piss this bird off, she goes, 'I prefer rabbit braised, if you must know, with herb crust and Bunratty mead. And basil *jus*.'

This bird, roysh, I think her name's Jade, she goes, 'I remember you from Mount Anville. You were in the class below me. You never got involved with Greenpeace or anything like that. The only thing you ever cared about was you. You certainly never cared about the planet, or issues, or …' Erika, roysh, she just looks her up and down again and she's like, 'Sorry, did the death of Linda McCartney open up a gap in the market that you're trying to fill?' Jade's like, 'You have one *serious* attitude problem. At least animals aren't just food to me. Or something to wear.'

And Erika, she always has to have the last word, roysh, she goes, 'Oh no, they're much, much more than that. They can also be used for testing cosmetics. Come on, Ross.' She goes into the shop and I, like, follow her in. What else could I do? I turned around to Jade, shrugged my shoulders and went, 'She got you there. You have to admit it.'

✻ ✻ ✻

My stash of CDs is, like, humungous now. A random taste: we're talking *Come On Over* by Shania Twain, we're talking *Be Yourself Tonight* by the Eurythmics, we're talking *Ocean Drive* by the Lighthouse Family, we're talking the soundtrack from *Coyote Ugly*, we're basically talking *Changing Faces* by Louise, we're talking *Never Stop the Alpenpop* by DJ Otzi, we're talking *Young Lust* by Aerosmith, we're talking *Full Circle* by Boyz II Men, we're talking *Panpipes – the Flight of the Condor*, we're talking basically *Gold – the Greatest Hits of Steps*, we're talking the soundtrack from *Notting Hill*, we're talking *Rise* by Gabrielle, we're talking *Tuesday Night Music Club* by Sheryl Crow, we're talking the soundtrack from *Moulin Rouge*. But I did not – despite what she's said to at least two people I know – steal *Step One* by S Club 7 from Ailish, as in Ailish LSB always in Lillies lives in Donnybrook Ailish. She focking *wishes*.

✻ ✻ ✻

The old man rings, roysh, and he's practically in tears. We're talking tears of happiness here. He's like, 'Get over here fast, Kicker. I've got a cheque for you.' I'm like, 'Have they gone?' He goes, 'The For Sale sign went up an hour ago. Ross, this is the happiest I've been since Castlerock won the …' I'm just like, 'Cut the focking pleasantries. This is business. I'll be up to you in an hour. Have the cheque written and ready for me when I get there.'

Which, of course, he doesn't, roysh, he's still farting around in the study, looking for his Mont Blanc pen when I arrive, which means I end up in the kitchen, listening to the old dear's bullshit. She's going, 'How are you keeping?' as if she gives a shit. I just, like, throw my eyes up to heaven, roysh, and go into the sitting room and turn on 'Dream Team'. Linda Block, love goddess.

The front doorbell rings and nobody answers it, roysh, and it rings, like, six or seven times and I end up having to get up from Harchester's vital UEFA Cup quarter-final clash to, like, go and see who it is. It turns out, roysh, it's, I don't know, whatever the fock the cream cracker next door calls himself, wanting to speak to the old man, or as he put it himself: 'Howiya bud, is your oul' fella in?' Slip-on shoes and a football manager jacket. The windfall's obviously done fock-all for the goy's dress sense.

I'm like, 'I'm sorry, I don't speak working class,' ripping the piss out of him, and I'm there, 'You'll have to speak slowly.' He goes, 'I'm, eh, looking for yisser fadder.' I'm like, 'Just caught the last word. I presume you're looking for my old man. I'll go and get him,' and I leave him on the doorstep, roysh, put the security chain on – you can't be too careful – and head into the study.

The old pair are there, the old dear's helping him look for the pen and I'm like, 'Is there something wrong with your ears or your legs?' The old dear's like, 'Sorry, Ross?' I'm like, 'The doorbell's been ringing for, like, ten minutes.' The old man's there, 'Didn't hear a thing, Ross,' and I'm like, 'Well you would have if you hadn't been listening to that dead bird so loud.' The old man's like, 'That's Eva Cassidy, Ross. She has a beautiful voice. Helps me when I'm working.' I'm like, 'Yeah, yeah, shut up, your best mate's at the door.'

I follow the old man out into the hall, roysh, just to get his reaction when he sees who it is. He sees the chain, roysh, and turns around and gives me this sort of, like, strange look. He has to slam the door in the goy's face first before he can take the chain off and, when he opens it again and he sees who it is, he goes, 'Hello, there,' then he turns around to me and he's like, 'The chain. Very good, Ross. You're thinking.' The goy's like, 'Alright, Charlie. What's the crack?' The old man just ignores this and goes, 'Well, what is it now? Not another lad of yours doing a sponsored walk to pay for the school heating oil?' He's like, 'Jaysus, no.' The old man goes, 'You're not planning to block out our daylight upstairs as well, are you, with a new, giant-sized pigeon loft, a sort of Ballymun, if you like, for your feathered vermin friends?' He's like, 'No, no. Actually, I've a bit of bad news for you, Charlie. Very bad news, as a matter of fact. Eh, we're moving out.' And the old man, roysh, goes, 'YES!' and shakes his fist at me.

The goy's like, 'It's a real pity, I know. We never got to go for that game of golf at that club of yours.' The old man's there, 'Shame.' The goy goes, 'A real pity. Sure herself was only saying the other night how well she gets on with your own missus. But, eh, don't think we're looking down our noses at you or anything but, eh, we just feel we don't fit in around here.' The old man goes, 'Doesn't have anything to do with the *foie gras* my wife sent in to you, does it?' He goes, 'What was that stuff?' The old man's like, 'It's a very expensive type of duck liver.' The goy's like, 'It brought all the kids out in hives.' The old man goes, 'Very rich, you see. Not used to it, I dare say.' The goy goes, 'Anyway, it's nothing to do with that. It's just … well, it's a lot of things. Sure the shop down the road doesn't even have the papers. The real papers. They only have the big ones. With the big gobstopper words. But sure they're no use for the sport.'

The old man goes, 'Yes, they're catering for their market, you see. People in this area love *The Irish Times*. Always have.' The goy goes, 'And then there's the off-licence. Sure they don't even sell my beer anymore. Or cider. She loves cider, you see. And the other thing is the telly. Can't get Sky Sports up here. The dish won't pick up the signal for some reason.' The old man goes, 'Foxrock, you see. It's very high up.' The goy goes, 'That's probably what it is. Listen, I better get in out of this rain. Catch me death, so I will. Just wanted you to be the first to know. Hope you weren't too upset when you saw the For Sale sign going up. Don't worry but. We'll stay in touch.'

'Yes, of course,' the old man goes, closing the door while the goy's still talking. Then he looks through the spyhole and when he's, like, disappeared out the gate, he turns around and goes, '*Yeeessss*!' He high-fives me and he goes, 'I think it was the *foie gras* that clinched it, Ross. Did you like that little detail? Your mother's idea.' I'm like, 'Don't give me that,' and I put this big lump of metal with, like, wires hanging out of it, into his hand. He goes, 'What in heavens is this?' I'm like, 'Don't know exactly. I broke it off his satellite dish last Sunday night.'

I tell him he owes me five grand. He goes back to his study to look for the pen.

✳ ✳ ✳

Me and Oisinn are in Club Knackery Doo and we meet the birds. Aoife asks me whether I've seen Sophie since she, like, came out of hospital. Me and Oisinn just look at each other and we both go, 'No,' at the same time, a little bit overeager actually, but she doesn't seem to, like, notice and shit. She goes, 'Ingrown toenail, my orse. I know a rhytidectomy when I see one.' I'm like,

'Really?' She goes, 'Oh my God, you SO wouldn't recognise the girl. I walked straight past her in Blue Eriu.' And Jayne with a y goes, 'It's weird. She was supposed to come out with us tonight, but when she found out you goys were going to be here …'

* * *

Aoife goes OH! MY! GOD! she is SO not looking forward to Christmas this year, roysh, because she SO knows that her points are going to go, like, totally off the scale, and we're talking TOTALLY here. Oisinn heads up to the bor to, like, get a round in while Aoife storts, like, counting up how many points she ended up eating last year. She's going, 'Two slices of turkey is, like, three points and it's, like, three for the ham, five for the roast potatoes, or seven given the amount of them my old dear ends up doing, and then Christmas cake is another five and pudding with, like, brandy butter is another, I don't know, seven. And that's not even counting drink.'

'And what about, like, sweets?' Emer goes. 'One Quality Street is, like, one-and-a-half. You could eat, like, twenty of those without realising.' And Aoife's like, 'Well *you* certainly could,' and Emer gives her this filthy, roysh, and Erika breaks it up, going, 'If I'd wanted to listen to bulimics and anorexics bitch-fighting, I'd have stayed home and watched 'Ally McBeal'.'

Oisinn, fat bastard and proud of it, roysh, he comes back with the pints, Ken for me and him, Miller for Fionn, and he goes, 'Which one of you is wearing DKNY?' Emer goes, 'I am, do you like it?' He sort of, like, sniffs her neck, roysh, and goes, 'An urban floral with accords of blood orange, tomato leaf, orchids and daffodils for a woman who appreciates the natural and the authentic,' and he says this in, like, a French accent. Emer goes, 'It is *such* a cool perfume,' and I think Oisinn's basically in there tonight if he wants to be, though I have to say, roysh, he's welcome to her. I'm with Fionn on this one: she's a focking bus stop with eye shadow.

Fionn is telling Aoife how he's basically pissing his way through second year psychology, roysh, and when the three birds go off to the jacks, he turns around to me and asks where JP is tonight. I'm like, 'He's still in a fouler with me.' He pushes his glasses up on his nose and he goes, 'Third week of the month, Ross. The boy's menstruating.' I'm there, 'No, we're not talking period costume dramas here. It's work stuff.' He goes, 'I have noticed a bit of tension there. Heard you're whupping his orse, saleswise.' I'm like, 'The goy just can't sell houses like I can.' Fionn high-fives me – I think he must have thought I said something else – then heads off.

Claire comes over then, roysh, and tells me she got a Christmas cord from Sorcha and an e-mail and a couple of text messages as well, and that her and Killian are, like, back together and they're *really* happy and, like, SO looking forward to their first Christmas in Australia, even though it's going to be TO-TALLY weird eating, like, turkey and ham when it's a hundred and ten degrees outside, and they'll probably end up actually having, like, a barbecue, maybe even down on Bondi, blah blah focking blah.

I just get up and walk off. It's, like, last orders at the bor and I still haven't copped off yet and though that wouldn't usually bother me, roysh, tonight for some reason I don't want to go home on my own. I spot Fionn chatting up Fiona, this Mountie who all the goys say is SO thick she carries ID around just to, like, remind her of her name. He's going, 'Personally, I lean more towards Jung than Freud,' which I must remember to slag him about later. I walk around the boozer a couple of times, roysh, and realise my options basically boil down to either Kelly, this complete psycho who I've been with twice, or Treasa, this total focking bunnyboiler who's only really here tonight because she knew I was going to be here. I end up going for Treasa. She might be flaky as fock but she's the image of Jennifer Connelly. She goes through the motions of pretending she's not interested, of course. She tells me I'm a total dickhead and bastard when it comes to women, but by the time she finishes her vodka and diet 7-Up, I've got her eating out of my hand. I head back to where we were sitting, roysh, to grab my jacket, and Oisinn goes, 'I see you've pulled Miss Cacharel again,' and I'm like, 'Beggars can't be choosers.'

Claire is asking Aoife what Mass she's going to on Wednesday morning, roysh, and Aoife and Erika just, like, look at each other and Aoife goes, '*Mass*?' Claire's like, 'Yeah, Mass. *Hello*? It's, like, Christmas Day.' And Erika goes, 'We've got loads of money, Claire. We don't *need* to be praying.'

✳ ✳ ✳

I'm on the way into work, roysh, feeling pretty shabby after last night, I have to say, and all of a sudden my phone rings and it's, like, this goy Eanna. He goes, 'Ross, I've got something to ask you. Don't bullshit me, man.' I'm like, 'Shoot.' He goes, 'Did you make a move on Melanie in Soho last week?' I'm like, 'Melanie as in LSB Melanie?' He goes, 'Melanie as in my FOCKING girlfriend Melanie.' I'm like, 'Hey, Eanna, I didn't know you two were married.' He goes, 'Asshole. You're supposed to be a mate of mine.' I'm just like, 'Deal with it,' and I snap my phone shut and turn up the radio. I focking *love* this song.

She doesn't know who I am.

And she doesn't give a damn about me.

Cos I'm just a teenage dirtbag, baby.

Yeah I'm just a teenage dirtbag, baby.

Listen to Iron Maiden maybe, with me.

✳ ✳ ✳

Treasa ends up doing a total focking *Fatal Attraction* on me again and we're pretty much talking TOTAL here. It's, like, three o'clock on Friday afternoon, roysh, and she's already rung me five times on the mobile and, like, three times in the office. Wouldn't mind, roysh, but she's not the only one whose calls I've been avoiding. The Timmonses, the couple I focked over with the house in Drimnagh, sorry Crumlin, have called, like, twenty times in the past three days, roysh, obviously trying to get me to change my mind, trying to shame me into selling it to them just because I agreed to. But the other goy offered more, roysh, and that's allowed. It's in the rules. Loaded, this goy was. Wanted it for his daughter as a Christmas present. He goes, 'It's so handy for the tennis club. I'll pay two hundred and fifty-five thousand for it.' I'm like, 'I don't know if I can. I've already given my word to ...' He's like, 'Go back on it and there's five grand in it for yourself.' I'm there, 'Five grand?' He goes, 'I'll write you a cheque now. Do I hyphenate your surname?'

Five grand is five grand, roysh, lets me pay off my credit cord bill and I've still got two grand left over to basically have the best Christmas ever, on the major lash. And just because it's Sale Agreed doesn't mean you've actually, like, agreed to sell the house to someone. But I am SO not in the mood to explain that to Alan and Margaret focking Timmons. I can do without the hassle.

✷ ✷ ✷

Another Friday, another nightclub queue. This bird who I don't recognise comes over, roysh, and says hi to Aoife and Amanda and it's, like, hugs and air-kisses all round and when she's gone, roysh, Amanda goes, 'Oh my God, that girl is *such* an asshole,' and Aoife's like, '*Hello?* Who are you telling? I was at the Horse Show last year as well, remember?'

Fionn tells me he met my old pair in town today, roysh, and they gave him a Christmas cord to give to me. I think about ripping the focking thing up straight away, roysh, but then I realise it isn't actually from them. There's, like, an Australian stamp on it, roysh, so I presume it's from Sorcha. I just, like, slip it into my pocket for later and we all move a couple of steps closer to the door.

One of the bouncers, roysh, he asks Erika how old she is and she just gives him this total filthy, roysh. He goes, 'Are you over twenty-one?' She goes, 'I was in Annabel's last night. I was in Lillies the night before. I wasn't asked for ID. What makes this place so special?' He goes, 'Jesus, love, don't lose the rag' – he's a total knacker – 'I have to ask you your age. It's door policy.' Erika goes, 'Have you been doing this job for long?' The goy's like, 'Eh, no. Me second night, love.' She goes, 'Well, you obviously don't know it very well. Bouncers only ask for ID to draw you into a conversation, to find out if you're working class. I think it's quite clear that I'm not working class, don't you?' He's like, 'Eh, yeah.' She goes, 'So let me in and stop making a focking nuisance of yourself.' And in she goes. Me and the goys are, like, breaking our shites laughing, roysh, when all of a sudden I become aware of this woman who's standing, like, next to me and just, like, staring at me. I'm like, 'Have you got a problem?' She goes, 'So this is the great Ross O'Carroll-Kelly, is it?' I'm like, 'Look, you're a bit old for me. Have you tried Leggs?' She goes, 'You don't have the first notion who I am, do you?' and I'm like, 'Nope,' and she goes, 'I'm Treasa's mum.' I'm like, 'Oh.' She goes, '*Oh* is right. I thought I told you to stay away from my daughter.' I'm just like, 'Takes two to tango.' She's there, 'I don't know *what* it is she sees in you. But she's promised me she's not going to go near you again.' I just laugh and I'm like, 'Hey, the girl can't help herself.'

She goes, 'Oh you're very clever, aren't you? All the answers. Well I can tell you if you ever come near her again you won't be dealing with me. You'll be dealing with Mister Penniworth-Brown.' All the goys are breaking their shites laughing at this, roysh, so I sort of have to play it real Jack the Lad. I'm like, 'Who?' She goes, 'Treasa's father. Of course, why would you know Treasa's second name?' I just shrug and go to walk off and she goes, 'Yes, off you go, into your nightclub. I just wanted to let you know that I've got one very sad girl at home.' I'm like, 'I already knew that,' and basically she has no answer to that, so she just tells me I'm a creep and she focks off, roysh, and everyone in the queue behind us storts, like, cheering and then, like, chanting, 'LE-GEND! LE-GEND! LE-GEND!' I head inside and have a couple of vodka and Red Bulls and get chatting to this bird Carragh, who used to be, like, deputy head girl in Dalkey. But I'm not in the mood anymore. After, like, half an hour, I fock off back to the gaff without telling anyone.

Fionn is out. The six loneliest words in the English language are Marks and Spencers' Meals For One.

✹ ✹ ✹

JP's old man drops my post on my desk, roysh, and it's basically the usual old stuff until I come to this one which has, like, the address handwritten on it, roysh, and PERSONAL written in the top left-hand corner and I don't recognise the writing. I open the envelope and pull out this, like, letter, which I unfold and go immediately to the signature at the bottom. And my blood runs cold, roysh, when I see that it's from Sophie.

I don't even read it, roysh, just lash it into my drawer and carry on opening up the rest of my post. It's mostly shite from solicitors, a bit of junk mail and a few letters of interest in the house on Stradbrook Road, which only went up for sale yesterday. But I just can't concentrate on my work, roysh. I'm just there thinking about the letter in the drawer and eventually I pull it out, roysh, and stuff it into the pocket of my suit and tell JP's old man I'm heading out for a coffee. He goes, 'Can you bring me back a cappuccino? And two chocolate muffins.' I'm like, 'Cool,' and he takes a long pull on his cigar, roysh, and he goes, 'Oh, and the little cute one with the blonde hair who works there. Bring me her.' And I make this noise, roysh, sort of like, 'Corrrr,' and I hate myself for doing it.

I head in for the coffees and the blonde one's not on, just this Chinese goy, and I order a large Americano and sit at this, like, table in the corner, switch off my phone and take out the letter, and it's like,

> Dear Ross,
>
> I've been planning to write this letter ever since that time in the hospital a few weeks ago, but I didn't know what it was I wanted to say. My counsellor

said that the best way to start is to tell you how you made me feel. I suppose the answer to that is: two inches tall.

I have an illness that's called Distorted Body Image Syndrome. The leaflets that the doctors gave me say it's a psychological disturbance that manifests in different ways, sometimes it's an aversion to food, other times it's just hating the way you look.

I've hated the way I looked since I was about fourteen. I thought my chin was too fat and my thighs as well. I hated the lines around my eyes and I hated my nose. I thought I knew the answer and I asked Mum and Dad to get me aug. for my 21st.

So there I was all bandaged up the night you and Oisinn came in to laugh at me – I knew it was you two, I recognised your voices. Imagine it, Ross. All your deepest little secrets and insecurities are laid out in the open for people to laugh at and then gossip about with their friends. I had to be sedated that night, you know.

I spent a week in hospital. And do you know what I discovered? When I took off the bandages and looked in the mirror, I still hated the way I looked. I still hated myself. In a way I should be thanking you, Ross, because that's when I decided that my problems weren't outside at all, they were inside. That's when I started seeing Jenny, my counsellor, who's helping me to get things in perspective.

I said I should be thanking you, but I'm not because I'm incapable of feeling anything but hate for you. Jenny says I should work on that too, because hatred is a negative emotion and those who feel it will never know anything other than bitterness. And bitterness just eats you up.

So I'm trying not to hate you, but I think you must be a very, very unhappy person to do what you did. I told Jenny that you treat everyone this way and she said that deep down you must be very, very sad.

I know you're probably going to show this letter around in the pub, but I don't care anymore. I'm learning to be happy with who I am.'

And at the end she's just signed it, 'Sophie'.

I fold it back up again really, like, carefully, slip it back into my inside pocket and I get up and leave. It's only when I'm back at my desk that I realise I didn't touch my coffee and I forgot to get JP's old man his. He doesn't notice, though. Too busy leching after Fionnuala, the new bird he hired this morning. I spend the afternoon basically spacing. At four o'clock I turn on my mobile and there's two messages. Michelle from Ulster Bank was wondering whether I've ever heard of Reserve 30. And Emma from Sutton wanted to tell me that she knows I took her Hootie and the Blowfish CD and I know damn well which one, she goes, we're talking *Cracked Rear View*, and she says she knows because JP told her and that makes me an asshole.

✳ ✳ ✳

Saturday morning I'm on Grafton Street, roysh, four days before Christmas and nothing bought. I'm walking out of, like, BT2 and who do I walk straight into, only Alan and Margaret focking Timmons. Big faces on them. I actually try to do a legger, but the goy's fast – wouldn't be surprised if he, like, played rugby – and we end up having this huge row on O'Connell Bridge. He's like, 'You double-crossing …' and I'm like, 'Hey, I'm not working today. I don't have to take this …' He goes, 'You sold our house to someone else.' I'm there, 'First of all, it was not *your* house. And second, no, it's not sold yet. It's still Sale Agreed.'

He has me by the scruff of the neck, roysh, and he goes, 'We've nowhere to live,' and I'm like, 'Look, the goy's coming in on Christmas Eve to sign. Midday. You up your offer to two hundred and sixty, throw ten in for me and it's yours. Can't say fairer than that.' He goes, 'WE DON'T HAVE THAT KIND OF MONEY.' I can hear Cliff Richard's voice coming out of Carroll's. I'd forgotten how much I focking hate Christmas music. The goy's like, 'Please. We've already given our notice in the place we're renting. We've got to be out tomorrow. We've nowhere to go for Christmas.'

All of a sudden, roysh, his wife catches up. She's all out of breath. The goy's like, 'Margaret, be careful. You shouldn't be running.' Then he looks at me, roysh, playing the sympathy cord, and goes, 'My wife's pregnant.' I'm just like, 'Well, I'm not taking the blame for that.' She's like, 'You bastard. We've nowhere to go. For Christmas.'

I'm wondering whether I should buy a new Helly Hansen fleece now or wait for, like, the sales. I'm there, 'Look, I'm actually shopping for my Christmas clothes. And you're making a bit of a show of me here.' He's there, 'Look at me. Look me in the eyes. You can't, can you? There's nothing in yours. They're dead.'

I hit the road, totally gone off the idea of shopping. Stop at the Shell garage on the Rock Road to, like, get petrol. There's this, like, massive queue and this bird comes in and tries to skip, going, 'I'm just paying for ten pounds worth of petrol. I've got the exact money.' I tell her to get to the back of the focking queue and she goes, 'Merry Christmas to you, too.' I get back on the road, roysh, and when I hit, like, Blackrock, I remember the cord from Sorcha that I got a few days ago and I pull into this, like, bus bay, get it out of my pocket and open it. It's like,

Dear Ross,

Well here I am, my first Christmas in Oz. It actually feels so weird to think that it's Christmas and I'm not going to see you. Alright, I'm a sap but that's my way of telling you that I miss you and am thinking about you. Merry Christmas.

I've been hearing so many good things about you. My dad said he met your mum in the Merrion Shopping Centre and the job is going really well for you. Are you still living with Fionn? Things are really happening for you and you so deserve it. You must be so proud of yourself.

Lots of love, Sorcha xxx.

I go back to the gaff and drink half a bottle of brandy.

✳ ✳ ✳

It's Christmas Eve morning and I'm, like, sitting at my desk, roysh, and basically the only thing I have to do today is, like, the paperwork on this gaff in Drimnagh, sorry Crumlin, and then it's, like, off on the major lash for me. There's a mountain of papers to be signed and, as we're going through it, I'm looking around the office, noticing that JP's old man, the complete lech, has got mistletoe hanging all over the place. There's a big, like, clump hanging over the photocopier, which the birds in the office are avoiding using. It takes about half an hour to get through all the paperwork and the signatures and then, finally, the house is sold and I don't have to, like, worry about it anymore.

I hand over the keys and I'm like, 'It's a really nice Christmas present for you.' Alan Timmons looks at me funny and he goes, 'Why did you change your mind? I mean, when you phoned us this morning, we thought you were trying to, you know, extort more money out of us.' I'm like, 'Well, we agreed a price and I'm a man of my ... no, forget that ... you're not going to be able to move in for a few days. Have you thought about where you're going to go? For Christmas Day?' Margaret goes, 'We haven't thought. A friend of mine from work's minding all our stuff. What there is of it. We might try and get a B&B. We're pretty stretched moneywise. Baby and everything.' I'm watching the door. JP's old man isn't in yet. I'm like, 'Look, I hope you don't mind, but I phoned around a few hotels this morning. See could I get you something. Most of them were full. The Four Seasons. The Burlington. I tried Jurys and they're, like, chocker as well, but, em ... there is room at the Inns.' Alan's like, 'We couldn't possibly afford ...' I pull an envelope out of my pocket and hand it to him. It's, like, the two grand I have left from the five I got from the dickhead who wanted the house for his daughter. I'm like, 'Don't argue. I owe it to you. Probably more as well. Merry Christmas.'

They get up and they're both like, 'Merry Christmas,' and JP's old man comes in, roysh, just as they're leaving, and I spend the next, like, half an hour staring into space, wondering what I'm going to tell him and this other penis who's coming in at twelve. Don't know what I'm going to tell him about his money either. JP's old man is saying to Sandra, one of the birds in the office, 'I'm an organ donor, you know. Do you want one?' And everyone in the office cracks up except me and eventually, roysh, he comes over to me and he's like, 'How're you doing, Ross?' I'm like, 'Good … em …' He goes, 'You don't have to lie to me. I know what you've done.' I'm like, 'You do?' He takes out a cigar and lights it. He's like, 'Conscience. It's a bad, bad thing to have. In this game anyway.'

I'm like, 'You don't sound, like, pissed off. I thought you'd go ballistic.' He goes, 'I blame myself. Should have watched you more closely. Especially this time of year. Christmas does funny things to some people. I'm going to have to let you go, you know that?' I'm there, 'I think I'm glad.' He goes, 'You're no good to me now. Like a champion racehorse with a broken leg. And you were. A champion racehorse, I mean. You were the best. You were Nijinsky, Ross. Nijinsky.' I'm like, 'There's one thing I've still got to do.' He goes, 'You're talking about your twelve o'clock, aren't you? Go on, get out of here. I'll handle him.' I'm like, 'He gave me five grand.' He goes, 'I expected as much. Don't worry. I'll cover it. We'll call it your redundancy.' I take a quick look around the room and as I'm walking out the door, roysh, he calls me back and goes, 'Hey, we sold houses together. We'll always have that, kid.'

I meet the goys for a few old scoops, but I don't, like, tell them the craic. JP will know soon enough. Oisinn says he was with one of the ugliest girls he's ever seen in his life last night in Howl at the Moon. He goes, 'I focking love *J'adore*. The fragrance that celebrates the rebirth of ultimate femininity, a sparkling, fresh, floral bouquet that expresses the outburst of a woman's inner emotions.'

I hit the bor to get my round in. Fionn tells Oisinn he's going to, like, help me carry the drinks, which is weird because we're all drinking, like, bottles. When we get up to the bor, I'm like, 'Fionn, I've a focking amazing idea. Let's go on the total lash today and, like, carry on drinking right through, we're talking Christmas Day, the lot. Me, you, Christian ...' He goes, 'I'm having Christmas at home. With my family.' The specky focker. I'm like, 'Oh, roysh. Yeah.' He goes, 'Me and Christian called you a taxi. Or a transport, as Christian calls it. We did it that time when you went to the jacks. It's outside. Go and see your old pair, Ross. They miss you.'

I don't actually remember the journey, roysh. The next thing I know I'm standing at the front door, staring at this, like, wreath that the old dear puts up every year, she got it from her mother, who got it from her mother, who got it from her mother. And I don't actually know whether I've rung the bell or not, but I must have done, roysh, because through the glass I can see someone coming, and the door opens, roysh, and it's the old man and he's like, 'Darling, come quickly. It's Ross ... look, it's Ross ... he's come home ... for Christmas.' And I just, like, burst out crying. I'm like, 'I've focked things up, Dad. Focked things up big-style.' He hugs me and goes, 'But we can put them right, son. We'll put them right.'

And next door, roysh, I can hear carols being sung and it's like,

Oh such a wonderful saviour,
To be born in a manger,
So that I can share His favour,
And my heart be made anew.

Listen to the trumpets,
Shouting through the darkness,
Crying 'Holy, Holy,'
The Night that Christ was born.

You know you SO want more, roysh!

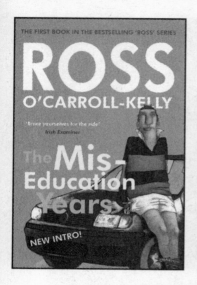
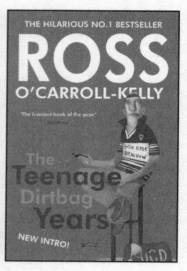
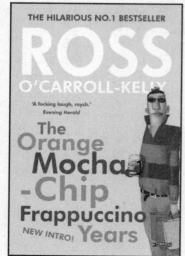
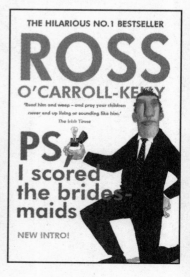